MURDER AT THE GEARHART

A Cedar Bay Cozy Mystery - Book 14

BY

DIANNE HARMAN

Published by: Dianne Harman
www.dianneharman.com

Interior, cover design and website by
Vivek Rajan

ISBN: 978-1719081573

CONTENTS

ACKNOWLEDGMENTS

The most common question I'm asked is "Where do you get the ideas for your books?"

The genesis of this book was kind of a no-brainer. My husband and I went to Gearhart, Oregon after seeing an article in the newspaper about how it was one of James Beard's favorite places. He'd spent a lot of time there, and the area was known for its seafood, which we both love. We stayed at the historic Gearhart Hotel, and my husband played golf at the oldest golf course west of the Mississippi.

When we arrived at the hotel and checked in, I noticed that they had posted a flyer regarding a James Beard dinner they were having in August. I inquired about it and found out that it was sold out. I've read a lot about James Beard, tried a number of his recipes, loved the hotel and the ambiance of that part of Oregon, and thus Murder at the Gearhart was born.

I can come up with the ideas for the books, but they'd never see the light of day without three very special people I rely on. My husband, Tom, who takes care of the house, the dog, and just about everything else! Vivek, who does all the technical things for my books, and who I'd be lost without. And Connie, who does the last spit and polish to ensure that no gremlins are left in the book when it's published.

Enjoy Murder at the Gearhart. Have fun with the James Beard recipes and thanks for reading it!

Win **FREE Paperbacks every week!**

Go to www.dianneharman.com/freepaperback.html and get your FREE copies of Dianne's books and favorite recipes immediately by signing up for her newsletter.

Once you've signed up for her newsletter you're eligible to win three paperbacks. One lucky winner is picked every week. Hurry before the offer ends!

PROLOGUE

This was Sam Jessup's big night. She'd made it to the top of her profession. For chefs who revered James Beard, anointed the "Dean of American cookery" by the New York Times, there was nothing bigger than being hired as the head chef for the prestigious James Beard dinner being held at the historic Gearhart Hotel. Finally, her time had come, and she'd earned it.

All those years of struggling to pay the bills, the toll it had taken on her life, an ex-husband, children she'd wanted but never had, her high blood pressure, and the extra pounds that came from being too fond of her own food, were worth it. Tonight, after the big event, she would allow herself to celebrate. This was her night to remember and nothing could take it away from her.

She smoothed her starched whites and tucked her hair into the stretchy hairnet that kept her coarse mane at bay. Her face was flushed with excitement for what lay ahead, unaware that her moment of glory would never come to pass.

Why? Dead chefs can't cook.

CHAPTER ONE

"Close your eyes, Kelly. I have a surprise for you." Mike steered her towards a kitchen chair and gently eased her down into it. "Sit down. This is an early birthday present for you. You can open your eyes now."

Kelly blinked, looking down at the envelope he'd placed on the kitchen table. The cream-colored envelope was inscribed with the words "Gearhart Hotel," which were located were under a small photo of an old-fashioned hotel. She looked up at Mike, surprise etched across her face.

"What is this? I've never heard of the Gearhart Hotel." She opened the envelope and pulled out a sheet of paper that was a reservation for two nights' stay in August, which was only six weeks away, and smiled. "I guess this means we're going to take a vacation."

"Look at the second page, Kelly." Mike was grinning like an excited child on Christmas morning just before the presents are opened.

She put the first piece of paper on the kitchen table and looked at the remaining page in her hand, reading it aloud.

"This is your admittance for two to the James Beard Dinner, a special dinner celebrating the life of James Beard. As 'America's First

Foodie,' he made an impression on chefs and food lovers that still reaches far and wide. No place was more important to him than the Oregon Coast and Gearhart, Oregon.

"Guests will be treated to a James Beard inspired dinner prepared by Chef Samantha Jessup, who not only studied with a protégé of Mr. Beard's here in Oregon but was also a James Beard chef award nominee. The dinner will consist of dishes using fresh and local ingredients from the immediate area. During dinner, guests will be treated to an exclusive showing of the award-winning documentary, 'America's First Foodie' presented by Producer and Director Beth Federici."

"Oh, Mike," Kelly said, her eyes lighting up. She put the James Beard information on the table. "This is like a dream come true. You know how much I respect James Beard. I mean, even though he's been dead for over thirty years, I think his old television shows are better than any other celebrity chef who's on television these days. I'm thrilled, but I'm really surprised. How did you ever think of something like this for my birthday?"

Mike sat down and said sheepishly, "I can't claim credit for it, although I wish I could. Your number one waitress at the coffee shop, Roxie, thought of it. One of your customers left a copy of The Oregonian newspaper at the coffee shop, and Roxie took it home with her. There was an article about this upcoming dinner at the Gearhart Hotel, and she thought, knowing how much you enjoy recipes by James Beard, to say nothing of your collection of his cookbooks, that this would make a great birthday present for you."

Kelly reached up to Mike and pulled him towards her for a kiss and a hug. "This is not only a great birthday present, it may just be the most wonderful one I've ever had. I still think his brownie crinkles are the best cookies I've ever eaten."

"Is that where your recipe came from? Every time I go to Kelly's Koffee Shop, I always order two of them. Didn't know that was a Beard recipe. They're wonderful."

2

"That's why they're on the menu. I think I'd have to close the coffee shop if I ever did away with them. The customers would probably start a protest movement to boycott the coffee shop."

Mike's eyes were gleaming. "Okay Kelly, now for the best part of the present. There is one more part to your gift, and I'm pretty happy with it, if I do say so myself. The chef who is in charge of cooking for the James Beard dinner is a woman whose name is Samantha Jessup, and she is evidently regarded as being one of the best chefs trained in the James Beard tradition in the United States. I actually talked to her after I spoke with the manager, and, drum roll please…" he said smugly. "You are going to be her sous-chef for the evening."

Kelly looked at him, her mouth falling open.

"You have got to be kidding. Mike, did you tell her I owned a coffee shop in a small town here in Oregon?"

Mike rubbed his chin. "Well, not exactly. I told her you owned a restaurant, every cookbook that James Beard had ever written, and prepared recipes from those books at least once a month. Yes, I did do a little what I suppose you might call 'puffing' when I told her your restaurant was widely acclaimed and probably the most popular restaurant in this part of the Oregon coast. I didn't think she needed to know that the restaurant was a coffee shop in a small town."

"Thanks a lot, love," Kelly said sarcastically. "She's probably expecting some high-end fancy restaurant owner-chef, and instead, she'll get a middle-aged coffee shop owner from a podunk town." Her face fell. "I'm not sure that part of the gift is going to fly."

"Kelly, you underestimate yourself. You're the one who's always talking about signs. Well, I took it as a sign that your birthday falls on the same day as the dinner. It was meant to be."

"Easy for you to say, Sheriff. You're not the one who's going to make a fool of herself," Kelly huffed.

Mike put his fingers under her chin and forced her to look up at him. He smiled and said softly, "Darling, quit being so modest. You're an excellent cook, and anyone would be happy to have you as their sous-chef. This will be a birthday you'll never forget."

He was right about that. It was a birthday she would definitely never forget.

CHAPTER TWO

"I didn't expect to see you here this morning, Kelly." Roxie paused from cleaning the coffee shop counter. "Not only is your birthday today, but it's also your chance to be a sous-chef to a lah-di-dah James Beard award winning chef. Should be interesting," she said with a laugh.

She'd been Kelly's right-hand person at the coffee shop for several years, and Kelly was pretty sure the reason the coffee shop was always full was because people just loved to be around Roxie. She never forgot a name, a face, or whatever was going on in a customer's life. Her ever-friendly smile and dancing blue eyes were always a welcoming sight to the customers.

"You can say that again, Roxie." Kelly chewed her lip and then said, "I don't think I've never been this nervous. I just hope I don't drop some main dish or do something stupid. Anyway, we're leaving in a few minutes, and I just wanted to make sure you didn't have any last-minute questions."

Still holding the cleaning rag in her hand, Roxie placed her hand on her hips. "Kelly, how many times have I handled this place when you've been out of town? A lot, right, and I've never had a problem. Charlie is here as usual, and Madison is going to help me out as a special favor. Since she used to work here, she knows the routine. Believe me when I tell you that with this crew, your coffee shop is in good hands."

"Thanks, Roxie, I guess I've really got the jitters," Kelly said, twisting her hands.

"Try and relax. Just enjoy yourself. I want to hear every detail when you get back, and I also want you to see if you can get the recipes for some of the delicious dishes you'll be cooking. I'm sure we could put some of them to good use here."

"I'll try. I just hope tonight goes well. And I do want to thank you for telling Mike about it. It really is a big deal. About the biggest deal that's ever happened to me." Kelly said as she tried hard to muster a smile.

"Go. Mike just pulled up and don't worry. Madison told me she's staying at your house and taking care of Lady and Skyy, so your house, the dogs, and the coffee shop are fully taken care of. Relax and enjoy. You'll do great. Now give me a big hug and get out of here!" Roxie said as she pushed Kelly towards the door.

Kelly waved behind her and walked out to Mike's car, trying to think positive thoughts about the rest of the day and night.

*****

"Well, are you ready for the big event?" Mike said as he leaned over and opened the passenger door for Kelly.

"About as ready as I'm ever going to be. You said Gearhart was about two hours from here, right?" she asked, securing her seat belt.

"Maybe even less, depending on the traffic. I told the manager and the chef we'd check in, and then you'd go down to the kitchen and report for duty. The chef told me she had a staff of six helping her in the kitchen, plus four servers, and that the kitchen staff was going to do as much prep work as possible yesterday, so they'd be fresh for tonight. She said she was going to tell them they didn't need to report until 1:00 this afternoon. I told her you'd be in the kitchen no later than noon."

Kelly checked her watch. "That's seems about right. We have plenty of time in that case. I hope she's okay with my paper bag waist pants and T-shirt. I even bought a pair of Croc shoes, like the chefs wear on television." A nervous giggle escaped from her mouth. "Anyway, I wanted to wear something that was comfortable but that wouldn't seem like I was trying to be more than I am. Figured I didn't deserve to wear a chef's coat or a toque, you know, those tall white hats chefs wear? I brought a hairnet in case she wants me to wear one."

Mike checked his driver's side mirror and set off down the street. "Since you're going to be helping her in the kitchen, I can't believe she'd find fault with what you're wearing. It's not as if you're going to have anything to do with the dinner guests."

"Okay," she said, slightly mollified. "Mike, we've talked about me and the dinner, but what are you going to do this afternoon? I know you're planning on going to the dinner tonight. I thought we could go to Seaside tomorrow. That's where Beard had his cooking school, and I understand there are some great hole-in-the-wall restaurants in Seaside and Cannon Beach.

"Plus, there's supposed to be a beautiful park close by, the Ecola State Park. I'd like to go there and while we're in Cannon Beach, we can see Haystack Rock. I saw a picture of it once, and it looked like it just dramatically rose up out of the ocean. Thought it was something we'd probably want to see." She settled back in her seat, relaxing as they hit the open road.

"Couldn't agree more. It's your weekend, so we'll do whatever you want. As far as what I'm going to do this afternoon, I don't think I mentioned that there's a golf course there. I'm going to play it. It sounds kind of interesting. It's the oldest golf course west of the Mississippi. After my stellar rounds of golf in Sonoma, I couldn't resist it. Since you're going to be sous-chefing, I didn't think you'd mind."

Kelly turned around and checked on Rebel, her ninety-pound boxer dog, who was sound asleep on the back seat. "I'm glad you're going to do that. About the only time you get to play golf is when we're on vacation, because you're so busy as Beaver County Sheriff."

She turned towards Mike again. "To change the subject, I'm really glad the hotel allows dogs. We can walk Rebel when we get there, and then he'll probably sleep the rest of the afternoon while we're both gone. Would you walk him when you finish playing golf? We can both take him for a walk when I'm finished tonight."

"No problem. Like I said, this is your weekend." Mike reached over and patted her hand. "Your wish is my command."

CHAPTER THREE

An hour and a half later Mike pulled into the parking lot of the Gearhart Hotel. "When I read the article in the paper, it said the hotel was listed on the National Register of Historic Places, and I'm not surprised," Mike said as he looked at it.

The bricks on the old building were smooth with age, some crumbling in places, and a rose creeper climbed around the arched entrance. Miniature trees in pots stood on either side of the doorway, which had a plaque on one side declaring its historic status. The back side of the hotel looked out on a large green lawn. The hotel was on the jaded side of grand, and Kelly suspected it had seen better days, but liked the fact that it was welcoming rather than imposing. She'd visited plenty of posh venues where the lack of ambience had ruined this experience.

The owners of the hotel had built a second hotel next to it, kind of an overflow hotel, which was more modern, but still had on Oregon feel to it. It was grey with plantings surrounding it, and it, too, backed up to the vast green lawn.

"I agree," Kelly said. "It looks like it definitely has been here awhile, and if the golf course is the first one west of the Mississippi, it has to be old." She stretched her arms and raised them, trying to loosen the tension in her shoulders.

She continued, "I'm kind of surprised they allow dogs and are only charging us $15.00 a night for Rebel. Poor guy's getting old, so I figured he could use a little time alone with us. Lady and Skyy make sure he doesn't get as much rest as he probably needs."

"I'll definitely second that for Skyy. She's got more energy than four dogs combined, and she's well past the puppy stage. Looks like that energy of hers is here to stay. I think we should take Rebel for a walk before we check in. The usual check-in time is 3:00, but since you're the sous-chef, they're letting us have an early check-in. Actually, Kelly, I could get used to the perks I might get from having you be famous." He chuckled as he got out of the car and opened the back door for Rebel.

Kelly climbed out of her side. "This will be fleeting, so don't get used to it." She pointed to the side of the hotel. "Look Mike, I'm impressed. They even have dog stations where you can get plastic bags. That's pretty thoughtful."

"I rather doubt they were doing it in the spirit of generosity, Kelly. I would imagine it cuts down on the maintenance for the grassy area."

"Hadn't thought of that, but I bet you're right. Mike, this parking lot is pretty full. Do you think they're here for the dinner tonight?"

Mike gave a slow nod. "I wouldn't be surprised. When I made the reservation, the manager said we were getting the last available room at the hotel, and that the surrounding hotels and motels were filling up because of the dinner. I was glad I called when I did."

They took a leisurely stroll with Rebel through the mature gardens, a leafy pathway leading them in a twisty circle through the grounds and back to the parking lot. After they'd put Rebel back in the car they walked into the hotel and over to the small registration desk.

"May I help you?" the young woman with the name tag of Dakota asked.

Mike spoke up. "Yes, we're the Reynolds, and we have a reservation for two nights."

"I'm sorry, sir, but the registration check-in time for guests is 3:00. I'm afraid you're a little early, but I encourage you to explore Gearhart or maybe drive down to Seaside or Cannon Beach."

"Yes, I realize that, but the manager said we'd be allowed to check in early since Mrs. Reynolds is helping Chef Jessup prepare the James Beard dinner tonight."

"I'm sorry, I remember now. Matt told me you'd be checking in early." Dakota shuffled some cards and handed one to Mike across the desk. "Please fill out this registration form. I'll need a credit card and a photo ID."

Mike completed the form and handed her his driver's license and credit card. "You'll notice that I filled in the section indicating that we have a dog who will be staying in our room, and I assume you'll add that charge to our bill," he said. "I paid for one night with my credit card when I made the reservation."

"Yes, sir. I have that information. As a matter of fact, a wire dog kennel has already been placed in your room. Here are your keys. Your room is one of only two in the hotel with a balcony, and it overlooks the back lawn as well as the golf course. We thought you'd like to be able see where the dinner is going to be held on the lawn. Just take the stairs or the elevator, and it's on the second floor, second room on the right."

"Thanks Dakota, I have a reservation for the dinner, so I'll be attending it. I think we'll go up to the room now. How would my wife get to the kitchen? She's scheduled to meet Chef Jessup there at 12:00, so the chef can tell my wife what she wants her to do before the rest of the kitchen staff arrives."

Dakota's smile never faltered as she gave them directions to the kitchen. "We hope you enjoy your stay, and if there's anything we can do to make your stay more enjoyable, please let us know. By the way, if you're hungry, you'll have to go into town to eat. The restaurant is closed for lunch because of the dinner tonight. The chef insisted on it, because she didn't want any distractions interrupting the prep."

"Thank you, and I think her request is perfectly reasonable," Mike said, turning to Kelly. "Tell you what. I'll walk up to the room with you. I brought in your bag, so you can freshen up, then I'll go back out for Rebel and the other bag. Ready?" He gave her a reassuring wink.

"As ready as I'm ever going to be. Since you've got the bag, let's use the elevator."

Mike led the way, and a few moments later he unlocked the door to their room. When he entered the room, he set her bag down on the floor and strode across the room to the glass door which led to a small narrow balcony. He stopped outside and inhaled. "Kelly, you must come over here, the view is beautiful. No wonder they wanted to have the Beard dinner on the lawn. Looks like they're setting up now."

Kelly followed him out onto the balcony and looked out at the green lawn and the tables and chairs that were being arranged on it. A man who seemed to be in charge was showing the rental company employees where to place them. Kelly noticed a worker with an armload of what appeared to be white linens walking down the small ramp from the back of a large rental event truck.

"Looks like it's going to be a pretty swank affair," Kelly said. She reached for Mike's hand. "Now I'm even more nervous, as if that's possible. See, I'm shaking. In some ways I wish I was just going to be a guest, but it will be fun to be behind-the-scenes at such a prestigious event. It should really be interesting. I'll probably be gone when you get back. I'm going to wash up and then head down to the kitchen." She looked up at her husband and lightly kissed his cheek. "Wish me luck. See you after the event. I love you."

"Love you too, birthday girl." Mike gave her hand a squeeze before letting it go. "Look at it this way, Kelly, even if something does happen while you're sous-chefing, you'll never have to see Chef Jessup again."

Later, he would realize just how prophetic those words had been.

CHAPTER FOUR

Kelly walked down the stairs to the lower level of the hotel where the restaurant was located. The restaurant was dark, but Dakota had told them it was closed because of the Beard dinner. She walked through the seating area of the restaurant to the kitchen, which from the directions she had been given, was through the door located at the rear of the restaurant. She knocked on the door, but there was no answer. She tried again with the same luck. Finally, she opened the door and walked into the kitchen.

"Chef Jessup, are you here? I'm Kelly Reynolds and my husband spoke with you about me helping you tonight," she said, her voice sounding stronger than she felt inside. A swarm of butterflies had landed in her stomach and she swallowed, trying to keep them at bay.

The kitchen was deserted. No one answered Kelly's call. She thought the chef might be in the walk-in refrigerator and crossed the room and opened the heavy stainless-steel door of the large commercial refrigerator. It was a reminder of how she wished Kelly's Koffee Shop's kitchen had room for a refrigerator that large. It was a constant battle to fit the items that needed to be kept cool into the residential size refrigerator in the coffee shop. Her solution was to keep a large cooler in the storeroom at the coffee shop for those times when she needed extra refrigerator space.

After she pulled the door open she stood in amazement at the amount of food that had been prepared and stacked on the shelves in readiness for the Beard dinner. The overflow of food and ingredients was carefully piled up on the floor. She looked at the boxes of food and knew that it was going to take a lot of work to get them ready for the dinner.

Several stacked boxes of beets were at an odd angle, and she was afraid they'd fall and make a mess on the floor. She knew it would be difficult to get the food out with them blocking the way. When she pushed them back towards the shelving, she looked down and froze. The first thing that struck her was how odd it was that a shoe was in the refrigerator.

"What the…" Kelly muttered. She took two steps towards it to see why it was there before taking another step back. The shoe was attached to a foot which belonged to a woman's body wearing traditional black and white chef's striped pants. The body was face down on the floor, and a large kitchen knife was sticking out of her back. Blood covered her white chef's jacket, and red splatters were visible on some of the food packets nearby.

Kelly recoiled in horror, realizing the body must be Chef Jessup and that someone had killed her. Adrenaline silenced the butterflies, and she bent down and put her index and middle fingers on the woman's neck to see if there was a pulse. There was none. She backed out of the refrigerator, closed the door, ran through the kitchen, and raced up the stairs to the reception desk.

At the reception desk, she struggled for breath. "Dakota, call 911," she gasped. "There's a body in the refrigerator, a dead body. I think it might be Chef Jessup." Her voice was urgent, and as her words registered with the young woman who had checked them in only a few minutes earlier, Kelly noticed that her fingers were trembling as she dialed 911.

When she was finished with the call, Dakota said, "I'll be back in a minute. I need to get the manager, Matt Parker. He's on the lawn, directing the set up for tonight."

Moments later the police chief and his sergeant rushed into the lobby just as a man hurried in from the back of the hotel. "Hi, Chief," the man said. "Mrs. Reynolds told Dakota that she found a body in the refrigerator, and she thought it was Chef Jessup. Come this way." He rushed in the direction of the stairs Kelly had just come up.

"Mrs. Reynolds, I'm Kyle Barnes, the Gearhart Chief of Police. Please come with us. I'll need to take a statement from you," the chief said, motioning towards the staircase.

Downstairs, as they were hurrying through the kitchen, the harried-looking man introduced himself. "Mrs. Reynolds, I'm Matt Parker, the hotel manager. I hope you're wrong about what you saw."

"Me, too," Kelly said, struggling to keep up.

Matt opened the door to the large walk-in refrigerator, and the three men stepped into it, Kelly waiting outside. She had no wish to look at the body again. A moment later an ashen-faced Matt walked out. With a nod to Kelly, he said, "You were right. It's Chef Jessup, and she's dead." He walked over to the counter and sat on a stool, putting his head in his hands.

"Sorry, I need to think for a moment." Matt raked his hands through his hair. "We've got one hundred guests coming here in six hours, and they've all pre-paid. They were promised a gourmet meal and they expect one. All the food has been delivered per the chef's instructions. She had her staff come in yesterday and do the prep work. She told me they were coming back at 1:00 today to finish what couldn't be done earlier. I don't know what to do."

The chief and his sergeant walked out of the refrigerator, and the sergeant made a call while the chief turned to Kelly. "Mrs. Reynolds, please tell me how you discovered the body. I need to know if you moved or touched anything."

Kelly told him exactly what had happened. While she was telling him, the sergeant walked over and said, "Chief, the coroner is on his way. Said it should be about twenty minutes. I told him we'd leave the body where it is. I'm going back in to take photographs."

When Kelly finished telling the chief how she'd discovered the chef's body, she said, "If you don't mind, I'd like to call my husband. He's the Beaver County Sheriff. You may know him. His name is Mike Reynolds."

The chief grinned. "Small world. I know Mike. We've both attended several Oregon law enforcement conferences. I'd heard that he'd gotten married a couple of years ago. Congratulations. He's a good man."

"I think so, too," Kelly said. "Maybe I can get ahold of him before he goes out to play golf. Excuse me," she said, taking her phone from her purse. She clicked on Favorites and called her husband, but after six rings she was put through to his voicemail. She left a message for him to call her as soon as he received the message.

Matt got off the stool where he was sitting and walked over to where Kelly and the chief were standing. "Kyle," he said, "I've got a real problem. The James Beard dinner is scheduled for tonight. We've got one hundred guests coming in a few hours, some of whom have even flown in for the event. Every hotel and motel in the area has been booked for weeks, and the reason they're full is because of the dinner. As we speak, the event rental company is setting up the tables and chairs as we speak, on the back lawn. This dinner has to come off. Our little city is depending on it. I've got an idea how to make it work, but I'll need help from both of you."

"Let's hear it, Matt." The chief rubbed his chin. "I know it's a big deal. Everyone's talking about it, and I've heard a lot of the business people in town say it's really been good for them. What's your proposal?"

"Well, it pretty much depends on Mrs. Reynolds." Matt glanced at Kelly. "Chef Jessup told me, that according to Mrs. Reynolds' husband, she's one of the top chefs on the Oregon Coast, and her restaurant is enormously popular. She's obviously qualified, so I'd like her to be the chef for the event. The staff was handpicked by Chef Jessup, and they've all worked with her in the past. Everything that could be done ahead of time has been done, and the staff is familiar with the recipes. At this point, I think all we really need is someone to oversee and be the point person if there are any questions or problems."

He paused for a moment to gauge Kelly's reaction. "Mrs. Reynolds, given the glowing recommendation given by your husband and the fact that Chef Jessup agreed to let you act as her sous-chef, it seems to me that you are entirely qualified to be the chef for tonight's Beard dinner. What do you say?"

I say I'd like to kill Mike about now, she thought, her face flushing.

She looked at him and said, "Please, call me Kelly. I would be happy to help you, but my husband's a sheriff, and I know how long it takes to investigate the scene of a crime. I don't see how we could prepare one hundred dinners while an active crime scene's being investigated."

"That was the next part of my proposition," Matt said. "Kyle, could you expedite this and let us have the refrigerator and kitchen back in an hour or so? I know it's a lot to ask, but this really is a big deal. Secondly, I'd like to request that no one be told of the chef's death until tomorrow. If word gets out, people either won't show up thinking the event has been cancelled, or they'll come here and demand their money back. We can issue a statement after the event is over."

The young sergeant, who had been silent until that point, spoke up. "Chief, the coroner should be here any minute. Even though his office is over in Tillamook, he was in Cannon Beach on another call, so we don't have to wait for him, if that helps in your decision."

The chief was quiet for several moments, and then he looked at Kelly. "Mrs. Reynolds, if you're willing to step up and do this, I suppose I can make sure that my team does the same. I'll need to call in a couple of other people to help, but yes, Matt, I'll give you my word that my people will be out of the kitchen so the chef's staff and Mrs. Reynolds can put on this event."

"I do have a request, Matt," Kelly said. "As I mentioned, my husband is a sheriff, and I've already left a message on his phone to call me as soon as he gets the message. I need to tell him what's happened."

"Kelly," Chief Barnes said, "I can speak for Matt. Yes, please tell him, and then have him call me at this number. Your husband's very well-respected in law enforcement circles, and if he would be willing to, I sure would like to use him as a sounding board and get his two cents worth while I try to figure out who killed Chef Jessup and why."

"Matt, Dakota already knows about this," Kelly continued. "Maybe she could keep an eye out for Mike when he comes in the hotel from golf and ask him to come to the kitchen."

"I'll tell her in just a moment." Matt handed Kelly a spiral-bound notebook that had been sitting on the edge of the countertop. "Kelly, here are the recipes for the dinner. You can familiarize yourself with them before the staff arrives. I suggest you hold a meeting and have each person tell you what they are supposed to do. I met Paul Nichols yesterday, and Chef Jessup said that Paul had been with her for years. He'll probably be pretty familiar with how to do everything. I think you could use him as your number one person.

"Dakota's the one who will be directing people to the lawn for the dinner," Matt continued, so I want to make sure she doesn't say anything about the chef's death. I'll be out in back, if you need me. Good luck," he said, hurrying out of the room.

As Matt walked out, a large burly man passed him on his way in. "Hi, Kyle, understand we've got a murder victim here. Where's the body?"

The chief took him by the arm and led him to the refrigerator. When the coroner had completed his examination, he and the sergeant placed the body of Samantha Jessup on a gurney and rolled it out to the waiting coroner's van. For the next forty-five minutes the kitchen and the refrigerator were filled with law enforcement personnel, but true to his word, promptly at 12:55, the chief and all of his investigative support staff left the kitchen.

CHAPTER FIVE

Kelly was looking at the recipes, trying to get a sense of what needed to be done first. She decided the appetizers should probably take precedence, followed by assembling the salad and getting the chicken ready. By then she hoped everyone would have partaken of the wines that were being served, gratis, by a well-known Oregon winery, so if there was a bit of a lag between courses, no one would pay much attention to it.

"Hello, I'm Paul Nichols," a voice said. She glanced up to where a man had stepped beside her. "You must be the chef that Sam told us about, the one whose husband persuaded Sam to let you serve as her sous-chef for your birthday." He looked around. "Where's Sam?"

Kelly was momentarily at a loss for words, but she felt the sooner she told the staff the truth, the easier it would be for all of them. She was just getting ready to tell Paul what had happened to Sam when the other five staff members showed up, two women and three men.

Kelly walked over to the kitchen door, closed it, and took a deep breath before she began to speak. "I'm Kelly Reynolds, and I'm afraid I'm the bearer of some very bad news. There is no way I can sugarcoat this. Chef Jessup was murdered here in the kitchen earlier today. The coroner and the police just left. I am so sorry. The hotel manager, Mr. Parker, has asked me to stand in for Chef Jessup this evening, and I have accepted his offer to be the chef for tonight's dinner."

She looked around at the six staff members, their faces registering every emotion from dismay to horror.

Paul was the first to speak, shaking his head as he did so. "No, she can't be dead. I was with her this morning, and she was giving me instructions on what she wanted done this afternoon. This is no reflection on you, Mrs. Reynolds, but she wasn't sure how proficient you would be in the kitchen, and she wanted to make sure that everything went smoothly for this dinner."

He stopped talking and put his head in his hands for a moment. It was apparent from the way everyone was looking at him, that not only had he been Chef Sam's go-to person, but he had the respect of every member of the hand-picked staff. When he looked up his eyes were shiny with unshed tears.

His mood seemed to change in a heartbeat. "What happened to Sam? Who did this to her?" He asked with tightly clenched fists.

Kelly noticed the shift from grief to anger and quickly answered him, before the others followed his lead and got caught up in his emotions. "We don't know. The police chief has started an investigation, and I'm sure that right now he and the others he called in to work on the case are trying to make sense of the photographs, fingerprints, DNA evidence they bagged up, and all the other things that go into finding a murderer."

"How was she killed?" The questions came from a woman who had the name Lena embroidered on her white chef's jacket.

Kelly hesitated for a moment before she answered, not sure if she would be giving away information that Chief Barnes would prefer wasn't released. She decided the chef's staff had a right to know.

"She was stabbed in the back with a chef's knife," Kelly said. The assembled group was silent for a moment, digesting what Kelly had just told them.

Paul cleared his throat, and his voice was ragged when he began to speak. "Look, guys, we've all been with Sam for years, and we know what a dedicated chef she was. Sure, she could be temperamental at times, but we all knew it was only because she was a perfectionist. That's what made her such a great chef. Let's put aside our feelings for now, and as a tribute to her, prepare the best dinner ever prepared in James Beard's honor. Let's give the people what they paid for. We can grieve, and I know we all will, but let's save it for later. Are you with me?"

Five voices instantly answered in the affirmative, and Paul's expression brightened. "Okay, yesterday Sam went over what she wanted each of us to do today. Let's get started." He turned to Kelly and said in a respectful tone, "Do you want to add anything?"

"No." She held up the notebook. "I looked over the recipes, and I think the best thing I can do is stay out of everyone's way. I'm here if you need something. I will be looking over your shoulders to ensure that everything is going smoothly, but I think Paul can probably answer any questions that come up better than I can. Thank you for being so professional."

The next few hours went by in a blur as the staff, cut, mixed, cooked, assembled, and plated the different dishes that were on the menu. Paul was overseeing the preparation of the main dish, the garlic chicken, along with giving instructions to people and answering questions. Kelly could see why Sam's restaurant in Portland was so highly regarded. Her staff worked together seamlessly and in unison.

A half hour before the guests were expected, there was a knock on the kitchen door. Kelly walked over to it, not wanting the staff to be interrupted, since each one of them was intent on his or her part of the dinner preparation. She opened the door and saw Mike standing there with a concerned look on his face.

She stepped out into the restaurant seating area, not wanting her conversation with Mike to distract any of the staff. The door swung closed behind her.

CHAPTER SIX

"Kelly, Dakota stopped me as was I getting ready to walk up the stairs. She told me what happened earlier and that the dinner was going to go on as scheduled with you acting as the emergency stand-in chef. Are you all right?"

"Yes, Mike, I'm fine, and the staff has been wonderful." Kelly gave him a tired smile. "They're true professionals, and everything's under control. I have the sense they were a very close group. In fact, Paul, who's evidently her next-in-command, asked the rest of the staff to do the best job they could as a fitting tribute to her, knowing her love for James Beard."

"The three men I joined for golf are all attending it. The hotel is really busy. Can I do something to help?"

"Yes. Please take Rebel for a walk. You've got time before the dinner. Oh, I almost forgot. The police chief here in town is Kyle Barnes. He says he knows you, and he'd like your input as he starts the murder investigation. He asked you to call him." She reached into the pocket of her pants. "Here's his card," she said, handing it to him.

"Well, if I'm going to walk Rebel, call the chief, and change clothes for the Beard dinner, I better get started. I'll see you afterwards. I'm sorry this happened on your birthday. I really wanted it to be special time for you." He squeezed her shoulders and kissed her lightly.

"Believe me, it's one I will never forget. Actually, even under these circumstances, I've enjoyed being in the kitchen and seeing how professionals from a top restaurant work. It's been an eye-opening experience, although it wouldn't work in my little coffee shop." Kelly glanced around at the sound of voices coming from the kitchen. "I have to go, Mike. I don't want the staff to think I'm slacking off. See you later." She turned and walked back into the kitchen.

"Kelly," Paul said. "We're ready to send out the first wave of appetizers. Some will be passed by the servers, and some will be on the tables where the wine will be served. I'd like you to take a look at them before they go out and see if we've missed anything."

As if, Kelly thought. *This staff has probably forgotten more about fine restaurant food than I've ever learned. Nice guy. He sure didn't need to say that.*

Kelly walked over to where the appetizers had been plated. She recognized several of them from the James Beard cookbooks she owned, such as the chopped liver in the shape of a heart, the smoked salmon pizzas, and the deviled eggs. The platters had been garnished beautifully and professionally. She decided that the guests and their palates were definitely going to get their money's worth at tonight's dinner.

"This looks wonderful. Please go ahead and take it outside to the guests," she said to the servers. The staff members who were in charge of the appetizers began assembling the second wave, which would go out in twenty minutes. The tomato soup was simmering, and the salads were being assembled. Paul seemed to have the main course under control.

"Don't worry about dessert. It's been made and is in the refrigerator." Paul's voice was shaky as he spoke. "We're serving red velvet cake with cream cheese frosting. It was one of Beard's favorites. When Joe and Lena are finished with the appetizers they'll cut the cake, plate the individual pieces, and put them in the refrigerator until it's time to serve. That frosting doesn't work if it's at room temperature. I think we've got everything covered. Now it's just a matter of the finishing touches. I want this to be right for Sam," he said, a tear coursing down his cheek.

"I'm so sorry, Paul. Knowing how closely you and Chef Jessup worked together, I'm sure this is the hardest thing you've ever done. But from what I've read about her and her strong work ethic, this is what she'd want."

"Kelly, working with Sam was just the tip of the iceberg. You see, we've been living together for over a year, and we were planning on getting married next year. I feel like my life is over."

Kelly took a deep breath and said, "I didn't know that. I am so sorry you have to be here and go through this. Thankfully, it will be over pretty soon." She was interrupted by a knock on the kitchen door. "I'll get it, Paul. Just take a moment for yourself."

She walked over to the door and opened it. Standing in front of her was a large woman dressed completely in red, from her open-toed sandals and red nail polish, to the large red fedora hat she wore on her head. Her red face completed the look.

"I'm Jessica Cartland, the food critic for The Oregonian. I'd like to have a few words from Chef Jessup about tonight's dinner. Would you get her for me?" the woman asked.

Kelly had never heard of the woman, and had no idea what the relationship was between her and Sam. But she was smart enough to know that allowing someone from the press to have access to a place where someone had been murdered hours earlier would be a disaster.

"I'm sorry, but Chef Jessup is not to be interrupted while tonight's dinner is being prepared," Kelly said, mentally thinking that it wasn't exactly a lie. If Chef Jessup was alive, she was sure that she wouldn't want to be interrupted.

"I'll just take a few moments of her time." Jessica took a step forward. "I'm reviewing tonight's dinner for a piece I'm going to write about James Beard, and I'd really like to get a quote from her." Jessica put her foot next to the doorjamb, so that Kelly couldn't close the door on her.

"I'm very sorry, Ms. Cartland, but I've been instructed not to let anyone into the kitchen. Please go, we still have a lot of work to do."

Jessica leaned forward and peered behind Kelly into the kitchen. "Funny, I don't see Chef Jessup anywhere. Where is she?"

"She's probably in the refrigerator," Kelly said inwardly grimacing at her choice of words.

She was interrupted by Paul, who had come up behind her. "Jessica, get out of here. If Sam wouldn't let you into The Pampered Hamburger restaurant, she sure as heck wouldn't let you in here. Forget the quote and beat it." He pushed her foot away from the doorjamb with his own and slammed the door closed.

The strains of Jessica's high-pitched voice could easily be heard coming from the other side of the door. "When I do talk to Chef Jessup, I'll make sure she knows about this. You may regret it."

Deep lines etched across Paul's brow. "I probably shouldn't have done that, Kelly, but Sam hated her. She refused to have anything to do with her. She not only wouldn't let Jessica in her restaurant, Sam was personally responsible for a number of other chef-owned restaurants doing the same. Quite simply, they hated each other."

"Why?" Kelly asked. "I thought chefs wanted good reviews for their restaurants, and actively courted food critics."

"Some do, but not Sam. She found out a few years ago that Jessica had demanded payment from a restaurant for giving it a good review, which is completely unethical. Sam told several other chefs about it and they refused service to Jessica. That's why Jessica would do anything she could to ruin Sam."

"What do you think she's going to do when she finds out what happened to Chef Jessup?"

Paul raised an eyebrow. "Probably say something like it was Sam's bad karma, or in other words, she deserved it for deliberately trying to ruin people's reputations."

"Wow! With that kind of a background between them, why would she even try to talk to Chef Jessup?"

"I'm sure she was hoping, in a different kitchen, and given the importance of tonight's dinner, Sam might say a few words to her. She was probably planning on saying a few zingers to Sam and hope that she'd get angry and ruin the dinner. That's the kind of person she is." Paul turned back towards the stoves. "I need to finish up the chicken. When that's over, we can all breathe a sigh of relief."

Kelly couldn't believe how seamlessly the rest of the dinner went. Finally, all the courses had been served and each member of the staff had begun cleaning up their station or the area where they'd been preparing food. When each one was finished they said their goodbyes and left the kitchen, leaving Paul and Kelly alone for a few moments.

CHAPTER SEVEN

Bobby Lee picked up his phone and heard his secretary's voice on the other end of the line. "Mr. Lee, there's a Mr. Ferraro on the phone who wants to speak with you. Shall I put him through?"

"Yes, I'll talk to him."

A moment later a voice came on the line. "Bobby, it's Gino Ferraro. How are things in Gearhart? Like to hear they're going well, and that the room occupancy rate is 100%. You know that first payment is due next week. Just calling to remind you."

As if you needed to. It's all I've been thinking about.

"Doing well, Gino. We're not quite at 100%, but I'm confident we'll be there soon. I'm well aware of the payment that's coming up, and you can assure your partners that I'll meet my obligation," he said, hoping he sounded convincing.

What he thought was, *I can only meet that payment if a miracle takes place or pigs start flying. Neither of which is likely to happen.*

"Actually, Bobby, we've decided to send a couple of our boys to Gearhart to pick the payment up from you in person. That way it can't get lost in the mail or have some problem with the bank." Gino's hollow laugh grated on Bobby's already fragile nerves.

"They'll be at the Rotunda Hotel next week. Names are Dino and Lucci. They'll land in Portland, drive over to the coast to pick up the payment and then drive back to Portland, so you won't have to waste a room on them. Nice talking to you, Bobby." The line went dead, as Gino abruptly ended the call.

Bobby leaned back in his chair, looking out at the ocean from his office in his hotel. Or rather, it was partly his, since the majority of the money had come from friends of his brother's in Las Vegas. Bobby knew when he met Gino Ferraro and his partners that he was making a deal with the devil, but he didn't have a choice.

The six months he'd been given for the right of first refusal on the land where he wanted to build the Rotunda Hotel had almost ended, and he was getting desperate. He'd thought he could get money from Chinese investors, but they'd all turned him down. They didn't think a high-end hotel in this part of Oregon would be profitable. Now he wondered if they'd known something he hadn't, because it was beginning to look like they were right.

The one-hundred room Rotunda Hotel was on the beach in Gearhart, Oregon. Bobby had spared no expense in building it, from the grand marble floors to the little touches, like the daily fresh flowers in each guest room. It boasted a dining room run by a chef who many said would be the first one to receive a Michelin star in that part of Oregon. The infinity pool was breathtaking, and the spa hosted every type of treatment a discerning spa guest could want.

Frustrated, Bobby ran his hand through his hair, wondering why his hotel wasn't the success it deserved to be. The Oregonian newspaper had said it was unique and had given it a good review, although they did say the architectural style was a little different from what one usually saw on the Oregon Coast. Even so, the occupancy rate hovered around fifty percent, and that was not enough to afford him the income he needed to keep his new wife, Amanda, in the style to which she wanted to become accustomed.

Fortunately, he'd had the foresight to have a penthouse suite built for Amanda and him next to his office, which so far had kept her happy. That and her daily spa treatments, but he knew she'd soon tire of those, and begin looking for other ways to make her life more pleasurable. What those might be gave him cause for concern.

The occupancy rate certainly wasn't enough to allow him to pay back his Las Vegas creditors, and that was a nice way of putting it. When he went to the money men in Las Vegas, he told them he was sure he would have a constant occupancy rate of seventy-five percent because of the location of the hotel and the uniqueness of what he planned to offer the guests. There was simply nothing like it in that part of Oregon, or anywhere else that he was aware of.

Now the time to pay the piper was fast approaching, and Bobby Lee knew the men Gino was sending could do horrible things to him if he didn't have the money. Gino had never introduced him to the bodyguards that always flanked the other investors and him, but Bobby had secretly hoped he'd never meet one in a dark alley. Now they were coming to his hotel to get the money he didn't have. He loosened his tie and opened the top button of his shirt which was constricting his shallow breathing.

His mother had often quoted the Chinese saying, "The longer the night, the more dreams there will be." Right then he felt he could use some dreams, because the last few nights had been sleepless and very, very long. Even Amanda's lush body hadn't been a distraction, and that was another thing that was concerning him. Amanda had physical desires, and she made sure he was well aware of them. What she wasn't aware of was that the fear that was engulfing him on a daily basis had reduced his physical desires to zero.

He thought about what the local banker, Nat Smith, had said when he'd gone to him to ask for funds to build the hotel. He'd told Bobby to go look at the type of tourists that stayed in Cannon Beach, which was only a few miles south of Gearhart. His advice to Bobby had been that the area only attracted families with children and they wanted to stay in hotels that were close to the kid-oriented shops and play areas. Nat had rejected his loan application, saying that Bobby's plans for the Rotunda were far too pretentious for the area, and quite honestly, a little odd.

In Nat's opinion, the Willamette Valley, with all of its high-priced pinot noir wines that attracted wealthy people, was a far better fit for the hotel plans Bobby had presented to him. He said he thought some of those people might appreciate Bobby's architectural style. Now Bobby wondered if Nat had been right. Maybe his hotel was too grandiose and different for the area, but he still felt that it could attract people who wanted a luxury hotel in that area. The only other hotel of any consequence was the Gearhart Hotel located across the street and down a block.

Even though it was listed on the National Register of Historic Places and had a golf course, the Gearhart Hotel's accommodations couldn't begin to compare with the Rotunda Hotel. What Bobby couldn't fathom was that somehow, month after month, year after year, it was booked solid, including the second hotel they'd built on the grounds.

To add insult to injury, it was the hotel that been selected to host the James Beard Dinner the following week, which was quite a coup. Bobby's restaurant at the hotel had applied to host it, but he'd been turned down. He'd thought if he could host the dinner it would bring people to his hotel and give it the boost it needed to make it profitable.

While he sat there contemplating his dire future, a thought occurred to him. What if something happened during the scheduled dinner? What if the chef the Gearhart Hotel had hired to prepare the special dinner, Samantha Jessup, died, and the hotel wouldn't be able to host the dinner?

The guests would be furious, and Bobby could step forward and offer the guests a discount to stay at his hotel. He could say he was trying to help out the hotel, sort of like a knight in shining armor. People would no longer want to stay at a hotel where a prominent person had been murdered. The bad publicity attached to the Gearhart Hotel would give the Rotunda Hotel the attention it needed.

The more Bobby thought about it, the better the plan sounded to him. Bobby knew he couldn't get his hands dirty, but he was pretty sure he knew someone who could take care of getting rid of Chef Jessup, someone who already hated her. He thought that sometimes family ties are good to have.

When the person he had in mind answered his call he said, "It's Bobby. I need a favor, but it's one I think will make your life easier. I know how much you hate Samantha Jessup, and I will make this well worth your while…"

*****

Andres Ramirez left the spa and walked through the hotel to the elevator, intent on going to Bobby Lee's office and asking for a raise. In the other spas where Andres had worked, there had been a spa manager, who took care of things like employee problems and raises.

Kind of fits, Andres thought, *since this hotel is going nowhere fast. I need to get some dough so I can convince Amanda to go to Columbia with me. Once I'm there I can get all the money I'll ever need.*

After all, when your uncle had been part of the Medellin drug cartel in the 1980's running their South American operations, and was still at large, all the family members knew he had more money sitting in offshore accounts than he could probably ever spend.

Andres stepped off the elevator and stopped outside of Bobby's office, his hand on the doorknob. He heard Bobby's voice talking to someone named Alex and hesitated. Probably that weird nephew of his who came to the spa whenever he was in town. He stood there for several minutes, absorbing the conversation he wasn't supposed to hear.

When Bobby hung up the phone, a smile lit up Andres' face.

No need to ask for that raise. When the deed is done I'll just tell Bobby I know all about it because I was standing outside his office while he was arranging the murder, but I might forget what I know for a certain amount of money. Yes, it's kind of like blackmail but so what?

Rather imagine he'll pay whatever I ask to keep him and his nephew out of prison. Think it was Garret Hedlund who did that song "Timing is Everything." And if this wasn't the best timing in the world, I don't know what is! This is going to solve all my problems. Amanda, sweetheart, time to extend those massage hours, like permanently.

Andres turned silently back in the direction of the elevator. *Never did like Bobby Lee. This hotel is history, anyway, and the icing on the cake is that Amanda's husband is actually going to make it possible for me to keep her in champagne and roses. I never could have imagined something this good would happen out of the clear blue. Yeah, some days you just get lucky, and today was my day!*

Andres returned to the spa with a spring in his step, amazed at his good fortune and waiting for the following Friday night. He wondered if the murder would be announced immediately or if they'd wait a few hours until the next of kin was notified.

What he didn't count on was that no statement of the murder was going to be given to the public.

CHAPTER EIGHT

Once everyone had left, Paul and Kelly sat down at the kitchen counter, tired after standing for so many hours. "Kelly, I'm beat, and I'm sure you are, too," Paul said. "Let's have a glass of wine."

"Sounds good. I noticed that the servers brought in the bottles that had been opened and put them on the restaurant bar. I'll get each of us a glass, using the wine from those opened bottles. You sit here and try to relax." When she returned, she handed him a glass and said, "Are you driving back to Portland tonight?"

Paul shook his head. "No, one of the provisions of the Beard dinner agreement was that Sam and I would spend last night and tonight at the hotel. We checked in yesterday and were planning on going back to Portland tomorrow in time for the dinner service at The Pampered Hamburger."

"Paul, I've read excellent reviews of the restaurant, but I've always been curious as to the name." Kelly took a sip of her wine, savoring the flavor of the crisp, fruity, young Riesling. "Where did it come from?"

"Very simple. Hamburgers were James Beard's favorite dish. Sam gave the restaurant its name as a tribute to him."

"Did you ever meet his protégé?" Kelly asked, curious as to what her cooking idol was like as well as his protégé.

"No. I'm from the East Coast, and both of them had died before I moved to the West Coast about ten years ago. I worked at several restaurants in San Francisco and made my way up to Portland. Sam was just getting ready to open her restaurant and was interviewing people to work there. I got a job in her kitchen and quickly moved up the ranks to become her sous-chef. She got divorced, and she and I got together. That's the short version…"

He cocked his head and stopped talking when they heard a knock on the door. "I've got it this time," Paul said, rising from his stool. He walked over to the door and opened it.

Mike was standing there. "I'm Mike Reynolds," he said, "Kelly's husband. Okay if I come in?"

"Sure," Paul said opening the door and putting out his hand. "I'm Paul Nichols. Kelly and I just finished up and were talking." They walked over to the counter where Kelly was seated.

Mike kissed her cheek and pulled out a stool. "Mind if I sit down? I'd like to talk to both of you."

They nodded and a moment later Mike said, "First of all, your dinner was a huge success. Everyone was talking about how it was the best meal they'd ever eaten, so you pulled it off beautifully."

"Good, the staff really kicked in. Given the circumstances, I was just hoping we could do it," Paul said with a sad smile. "Would you like to join us for a glass of wine, Mike?"

Mike shook his head.

Kelly stared at her husband. "Thanks, Mike. I thought it went very well, but why do I get the feeling you came here with more to tell us than that we did a good job?" she asked, her eyes narrowing.

"Because I did. I have a couple of things to tell you." Mike looked at each of them in turn. "First of all, while the waiters were removing the dessert plates from the tables, the manager of the hotel, Matt Parker, thanked everyone for coming and said the dinner had been so well received that the hotel expected to make it an annual event, and he hoped the guests would all come back for it next year.

"But here's the interesting part. A large woman dressed in red with a red hat stood up and said, 'I'm sure all of us would personally like to thank Chef Jessup. Would you please ask her to come out?'"

"What did Matt say?" Kelly asked. "Poor guy. What a horrible position she put him in, whether she knew anything or not."

"He was brilliant. Talk about thinking on your feet. He said something to the effect that he had spoken with the chef a little earlier and asked if she'd be willing to come out of the kitchen for kudos, but she'd declined, saying she was really tired. Then he thanked everyone again for coming and started talking to people. The woman seemed angry, although I don't know why."

"I do," Kelly said. "I'll fill you in later. What else do you have to tell us?"

"It looks like you and I are going to have to try and solve the chef's murder," Mike said.

"What are you talking about?" Kelly asked in surprise. "I know the chief asked you to call him, but he told us he was going back to the station to begin working on the case immediately," she said.

"He did, but almost as soon as he got there his son's school called. He'd fallen during recess and bottom line is he hit his head on the concrete play area, and he's in a coma at the local hospital. Kyle said his first priority is his family, which is to be expected. He asked me if I would take over the investigation. He told me the Gearhart Police Department is quite small, and he didn't have anyone as qualified as me to conduct the investigation."

Kelly raised her hand to her mouth. "Oh, no. That poor man.

What's the prognosis for his son?"

"It's too soon to tell. He's having a number of tests done so they can assess his condition and see if he needs to be airlifted to the Doernbechere Children's Hospital in Portland. It has an excellent reputation, and they were going to make a decision, probably sometime tonight, based on the tests they were conducting."

"I understand you said you'd help with the investigation, but we were going to drive home Sunday. What are your plans now?"

"Kelly, I don't know," Mike sighed. "I'm going to spend tomorrow and Sunday investigating the case, and I'll just have to take it from there. I probably could take a day or two off and stay here, depending on what's happening at home. I need to check in with the station. If you have to get back, you could take the train."

Kelly had already made her mind up. "No, I'll stay with you. I guess what we need to do now is look for suspects. What you don't know is that Paul and Chef Jessup were planning on getting married." She turned to Paul. "Paul, I hate to ask this of you, but I've helped my husband solve several murder cases, and time is so important. In fact, there's a saying that law enforcement uses. It's called the '48 Hour Rule,' and what it means is that the chances of solving a crime diminish substantially after the 48-hour mark. Isn't that right, Mike?"

"Yes," Mike said, nodding, "and I think I know where Kelly's going with this. I'm sure you must be somewhat in shock, but can you think of anyone who would have a reason to murder Chef Jessup or wish her dead?"

Paul took a sip of wine and seemed to drift off into space for a few moments, as if trying to gather his thoughts before he spoke. He looked at Mike when he eventually spoke. "I've deliberately tried not to think of that. Right now, I'm all over the board with my emotions, and I don't want to accuse anyone of something as horrendous as murder. Can you understand that?"

"Yes, of course I can, and the feelings you're experiencing are perfectly natural. I'm not asking you to accuse anyone of murder. I'd just like to get some names of people you think might be of interest in that regard. Let's use that term. Can you think of anyone who would be of interest?" Mike asked.

"Well, I suppose the first person who comes to mind is her ex-husband, Ryan Stevenson," Paul said. "They met when they were both studying at Le Cordon Bleu in Portland. It's closed now, but for years it was a very prestigious school for people who wanted to become chefs.

"After they graduated, they got married and Sam worked as his sous-chef at the restaurant Ryan had opened. Sam decided she wanted to open her own restaurant, and Ryan was really against it. They had very different thoughts on what a successful restaurant should be. They'd been having problems for years and Sam finally said she'd had enough, and they got divorced. After they were divorced, Sam took back her maiden name. Interestingly, Ryan's restaurant, The Pioneer Grill, just off Pioneer Square in Portland, is very successful.

"A year or so after Sam opened her restaurant, The Oregonian referred to The Pampered Hamburger as the best restaurant in Portland and a tribute to the famous chef, James Beard, in honor of his favorite food. Naturally, that didn't sit well with Ryan, so I guess he could be considered a person of interest."

Mike was writing in the notebook he always carried with him. "Okay, Paul. Anyone else?"

"That woman who stood up at the end of dinner, Jessica Cartland, would sure be on my list. She and Sam hated each other. She tried to barge her way in here just before the dinner tonight. Kelly can tell you all about it later. She is definitely not a nice person."

"What about family? Did Sam have any children?"

"No. She told me she really had wanted to have children, but a chef/restaurant owner's hours were not conducive to parenting, particularly since her husband also had the same weird hours. As far as parents, etcetera, she was an only child. Her parents died several years ago. She told me once that she was kind of like one of those orphan cattle they call 'dogies.' She said she was the last of her family, since her mother and father were also only children. She might have some shirttail relatives somewhere, but if she did, she never mentioned them."

"Anyone else you can think of?" Mike asked.

"Not really." Paul paused, then added as an afterthought, "she did mention something one time about a chef in San Francisco who was angry with her because she wouldn't share her recipes with him. He told her it was considered to be a courtesy in the industry to do that. She told me she and he had studied together under James Beard's protégé in Cannon Beach.

"I remembered we laughed about it, saying we'd never heard of any such thing. Most chefs of successful restaurants tightly guard their recipes for their signature dishes for fear that some restaurateur will take the recipes, serve the dishes at their restaurant, and claim them as their own."

Mike tapped his pen on the notebook he had in his hand. "Do you remember his name? Matt said he'd get a list to me first thing in the morning with everyone's names who attended the event. I'd like to see if he's on the list."

"Let me think for a minute."

Paul looked up towards the ceiling and off to his left. Kelly watched him and remembered when she'd taken a class on body language several years ago, and the instructor had told the class that when people were trying to remember something, that's where they looked. The instructor had also told the class that when people looked up and to the right, there was a good chance that they were lying. She'd told Mike about it, and he said that had been his experience. He told her he always checked to see where someone was looking when he was talking to people, particularly if they were a person of interest.

"I think his name is Daniel Moore and the restaurant he owns is called Beard's Bistro, in honor of James Beard, which is why he wanted Sam's recipes. Maybe it's in her diary."

Mike and Kelly both looked at him, wide-eyed. Mike was the first to speak. "A diary. Sam kept a diary?"

"Yeah. She was really into it. Wrote every day. She'd never let me read it, and it became kind of a running joke between us. She wrote in it and then would make a big deal about putting it in her desk drawer when she was finished, and I'd make a big deal about walking over to her desk and telling her I was going to open the drawer and read it. We both knew I'd never do it, because I respected her wishes and her privacy. If she wanted to keep it a personal thing, that was fine with me."

"Paul, did she bring her diary with her when she came here?" Kelly asked.

He nodded. "Yes, she took it with her everywhere she went. Why?"

"I'll tell you why, Paul," Mike said. "This could be a critical part of the investigation. She could have written something in it about the person who murdered her. I'd really like to read it."

"I'm sorry, Mike, but I'm not comfortable with having you read it. If she wouldn't let me, her husband-to-be, read it, I'm sure she wouldn't want someone she'd never met to read it."

Mike was quiet for a few moments before continuing. "Paul, I completely understand what you're saying, and believe me, I respect your opinion. But I want you to think of her diary in another way. Respecting her wishes, you probably would get rid of her diary and never read it. Maybe you'd even burn it up, so no one else could ever read it. But what if that diary held the key to whoever murdered the woman you loved? You could be responsible for letting the murderer of your fiancée go free and never be caught. I don't think you'd want to have to live with that, would you?"

Paul sighed deeply. "You're putting me in an untenable situation, Sheriff. I really don't know what to say."

"If Kelly had been murdered, I would do everything in my power to find the person who did it, even if it meant that something of hers would no longer be private. When Chef Jessup told you she didn't want you to read it, I'm sure she never anticipated that she would be murdered, and I'd bet she'd want you to let me read it to see if it would help me find whoever did this to her."

Mike sat quietly while Paul thought about what he'd just said. "All right. I understand what you're saying. If it helps you find out who did it, I can live with turning it over to you, but I do have one request. I don't want whatever is in the diary to be made public. If you have to use its contents to find out who killed her, that's one thing, but I don't want it released to the press or anyone else. Can you promise me that?"

"Certainly, but since Kelly will be helping me, I'd like you to give her permission to read it. Would that be okay with you?"

"Yes, but no one else. I don't want it to be left on the police chief's desk so that anyone who walks by can look in it."

"Understood. I promise you that Kelly and I will be the only people who have access to it, and when we find the murderer, the diary will be destroyed by me. Can you live with that?"

"Yes. I'll go get it now. I'll be back in a few minutes." He stood up and left the kitchen, looking years older than he had when Kelly had met him several hours earlier.

Kelly's eyes followed Paul out of the room before she turned back to Mike. "Why don't we split this up when we get back to the room? It's late and about the only things we can do at this time of night is research a couple of names on the internet and read the diary. Why don't you take the internet, and I'll take the diary? We can start working tomorrow morning with whatever we find tonight. Sound okay to you?"

"Yeah, I feel bad about asking Paul for the diary, but it might very well hold a critical clue, and I can't overlook it."

A few minutes later Paul returned. He walked across the kitchen and handed Mike a red book. "Here's the diary. She actually started a new one every two years, but I think if there are any clues as to who murdered her, they would be in this one. She's been writing in it for at least a year and a half."

"I agree. Paul, I know you didn't want to do this, and I really appreciate it. I have a feeling the diary holds the key to the murder, although I have nothing to base that on. Try and get some sleep. Will you be around here tomorrow or are you leaving for Portland in the morning?" Mike asked.

"I think I better leave very early. The Pampered Hamburger was closed last night and tonight, but I noticed before we left that Saturday night was completely booked. Coupled with the fact that we'll probably get some publicity because of Sam's death, I imagine it will be a zoo. The staff is like a family, and I know this is really going to be hard on them. I need to be there to support them as well." Paul picked up his wine glass and drained the remainder of it.

"Funny," he continued, staring into the bottom of the empty glass, "but Sam and I had wills drawn up a couple of months ago in anticipation of getting married. I was the one who suggested it, because I inherited some property when my parents died, and I wanted to make sure that Sam got it. She willed the restaurant to me. Never in a million years did I think she would die before I did." He turned to Kelley with a forced smile on his face. "Kelly, it was nice working with you today. Thanks for all your help with the dinner. I wrote my cell phone on the back of this business card. Please let me know what you find out." He nodded at Mike and turned and walked out of the kitchen, tears flowing down his cheeks.

Kelly felt herself choking up. "Oh, Mike. This whole thing is so sad. My heart goes out to him. I know you always say to follow the money when there's been a murder, but I can't even begin to think he had anything to do with it, even if he will inherit the restaurant."

"I agree. It doesn't sound like he needs the money, and in time, his name probably would have been right up there with hers as a co-owner. No, I saw nothing that leads me to suspect he had anything to do with it. Let's go upstairs. Do you think we need to do anything other than turn off the lights?"

"Let me wash these wine glasses. The staff did a great job cleaning up, so I don't think anything else needs to be done. Be with you in a minute."

CHAPTER NINE

Daniel Moore ended the call and then began pacing rapidly around his small apartment. He couldn't believe that Sam Jessup, the little twerp he'd helped when they were taking classes from one of James Beard's protégés in Cannon Beach, Oregon, had turned him down when he'd asked her for the recipes the protégé had given her. Who would have ever thought she'd open up her own restaurant and become, as some said, "The female James Beard."

It was simply unfathomable. He could hear his father's voice in his ear, "Son, remember one thing. Women were put on this earth to serve men. We need them, but they are not equal to us." He remembered how his mother had always walked a little behind his father and waited until he spoke to her before she spoke.

He'd learned a lot from his father who was an elder in a very conservative church. He firmly believed that women were inferior to men and said that was why Adam came first. Because he was more important than Eve.

Daniel had been indoctrinated in male superiority at an early age, and now, as a man in his late thirties, he still believed it to be true. He'd never married, because the women he'd met didn't share his view of the role a woman should play in a marriage. Some day he knew he'd find a woman who would be content to play second fiddle to him, but so far, she hadn't materialized.

45

That's what made him even madder when Sam refused to give him her recipes. Didn't she know that the man was superior to the woman, and in this case, Daniel's restaurant was far more important than hers? The problem with that line of thinking was that she had the reputation of being the embodiment of James Beard and not him. Quite simply, that wasn't the way it was supposed to be. She should be a server, not a chef. That's why all the people who worked in his kitchen with him were male, and all the servers were women. That's the way it should be.

He thought it was probably his fault she'd gotten famous. She didn't even know how to crack an egg when he'd helped her all those years ago. Now he regretted it. She wouldn't even give him the recipes he wanted. Without him, she'd still be back in Cannon Beach, probably working in some fast food take-out joint.

Daniel had found out several years earlier that Sam had stayed in touch with the man they'd studied under, the protégé of James Beard, until his death. He'd heard that James Beard had given the man several recipes of his and made him promise he would pass them on only to someone he deemed worthy of them. Turned out it was Sam. Sam Jessup had made her reputation, and owned the finest restaurant in Portland, based on the recipes James Beard's protégé had given to her. It was not the way it should be.

He really didn't see what the big deal was. His restaurant was in San Francisco and wouldn't be in competition with hers, so why would she not share the recipes? No, it seemed to be sheer meanness on her part. It was like his father always said, "The world is full of sinners, of people who are evil, and don't do the right thing." In his mind, Sam Jessup was one of those. The right thing would have been to give Daniel the recipes he wanted. He'd wheedled, coaxed, and threatened her. All to no avail. She had steadfastly refused to give him the recipes.

To add insult to injury, when he'd found out on a webzine that the James Beard dinner was being held at the Gearhart Hotel and they were interviewing chefs to prepare the dinner, he'd immediately sent in his resumé. He'd waited several days, and after he'd heard nothing, he called some guy named Matt Parker, the manager of the hotel. The guy had informed him that the position had been filled by a chef named Samantha Jessup from Portland.

Just thinking back to that day made him see red all over again. She obviously didn't know her place, and he, a man, should be the chef for the event. As a matter of fact, he'd called her and told her that since she'd gotten the plum assignment and he hadn't, she owed him. He'd told her she could send him the recipes, and he'd consider the score even. She'd laughed at him, and that's when he'd lost it. She was laughing so hard she could barely talk when she told him to never contact her again or she would get a legal restraining order to keep him from contacting her. Then she'd hung up.

He recalled throwing plates at the wall, wishing it was Sam Jessup that had shattered and broken, instead of the plates. He knew he had to do something. His head felt like it was exploding. That's when he came up with his idea. If he couldn't have the recipes, then no one else should either. He'd make a reservation for the James Beard dinner and stay at the hotel. It was a perfectly plausible thing to do since he was known for cooking in the style of James Beard. No one would think twice about him attending a dinner in Beard's honor that was featuring his favorite foods. And if something happened to the chef just before the dinner, oh well. Accidents do happen.

CHAPTER TEN

"Mike, I'm going to get comfortable before I start on this project. It's been a long day, and I suggest you do the same." Kelly took a pair of pajamas and a terrycloth robe out of her suitcase.

"Good idea. It's already late, so let's plan on not working longer than a couple of hours. Tomorrow will probably be pretty busy," he said as he sat down at the desk in the room and plugged in his laptop computer.

Kelly got into the large king size bed, turned on the nightstand lamp, and opened the diary. She was a quarter of the way through it when she said, "Mike, I've found something."

"You're probably going to find a lot of things. Let's do this. I'll work with what I need to find out, and you keep reading the diary. Why don't you bookmark pages you feel might be relevant, and then we can both discuss what we've found out. Sound okay?"

"You're probably right. I was just kind of shocked when I discovered who I think could be a person of interest," she said.

"Hold the thought. I should be through in about an hour and from the looks of how much you've already read, you'll probably be through with it about then too." He turned back to his computer. They were both quiet, each concentrating on what they were doing.

An hour later Kelly said, "Mike, I just finished the diary, and I've found several people I think could be considered persons of interest. How about you?"

"I did some research on her ex-husband as well as Jessica Cartland and Ryan Moore. Do you want me to start or do you want to?" he asked.

"Why don't you go ahead?" Kelly said. "I think I'll make some notes while we're talking. It might help us prioritize what we need to do tomorrow. Oh, and I just had a thought. We've only got one car, and we each may need to go places. That could really slow us down."

"Sorry, Kelly. I got caught up in Paul's conversation after the dinner and forgot to mention to you that Chief Barnes told me he was calling the station and letting me have a car. He told me I could pick the key up from his sergeant tomorrow morning. No matter what we've found out tonight, I think that should be a priority tomorrow morning."

"Sure, right after I've had my coffee. I can guarantee you that nothing is going to happen until my caffeine level has been reached."

Mike came over and sat on the edge of the bed. "Trust me, Kelly, I'm well aware of that. In fact, I think anyone who's ever been around you first thing in the morning is well aware of that," he said with a grin.

"Thanks," she said sarcastically. "Okay, shoot. What have you found out?"

"I spent a lot of time researching Chef Jessup. I read pages and pages about how wonderful her restaurant is, where she got her training, yada, yada, yada. There were several mentions of her ex-husband and that they'd met when they were both students at Le Cordon Bleu in Portland, which is exactly what Paul told us. The article said she had been her husband's sous-chef. It went on to say that she'd opened her own restaurant.

"There was nothing in the material I read that would make me think her ex-husband might be involved in her murder, but you never know. There was a lot of stuff written about how she considered James Beard to be her muse, and that she had named her restaurant, The Pampered Hamburger, in honor of him and his favorite food.

"Of course, that doesn't mean her ex-husband wasn't the murderer. One of the articles hinted that Chef Ryan was not happy when her restaurant was named as the best in Portland, but that was about all I could find. I did check to see if he's remarried, but evidently he hasn't, because none of the articles mentioned it."

"What did you find out about Daniel Moore, the chef from San Francisco that Paul told us about?" Kelly asked.

"That was a little more interesting. The reviews of him and his restaurant were quite good, but I found something, while it doesn't relate to the murder, is kind of a red flag for me."

"What's that?" Kelly asked.

"Well, there was a bio of Chef Moore. Whoever wrote the bio mentioned that he'd been raised in a very, very conservative household. Evidently his father was an elder in some offshoot church that believed men were superior to women…" he said with a sideways look at her.

"Don't get any ideas, Sheriff," Kelly said. "That won't work in our household."

"Don't I know that?" he said. "Anyway, the article went on to say maybe that was why the chef had never married, since today's women did not believe in male superiority."

"Any references to Chef Jessup in the articles?" Kelly asked.

"Yes. One of the articles said that Chef Ryan had taken classes with Chef Jessup when they were both in their early twenties from a protégé of James Beard who taught in Cannon Beach. The article was a bit snarky, because it went on to say that it seemed the mantle of James Beard had been passed on to Chef Jessup through James Beard's protégé. It even mentioned that the protégé had given her the recipes James Beard had entrusted to him. Said it was too bad Chef Moore hadn't gotten the recipes, because then maybe he'd be recognized as the embodiment of James Beard instead of Chef Jessup. One other thing the article said was that Chef Moore had made the comment to several people that no woman should have James Beard's recipes, and the reason he'd said that was probably his upbringing."

"Sounds to me like a woman wrote the article," Kelly said.

"I'd have to agree. Let me tell you what I found out about Jessica Cartland, and then I have to send off a couple of emails to my staff back at the sheriff's office in Beaver County."

"Good. I could probably use a little break myself."

"Okay, on to Jessica. She wanted to become a chef and attended Le Cordon Bleu in Portland."

"Does that mean she studied with Ryan and Samantha? Maybe that's where the animosity between the two women began," Kelly pondered.

"No, she was there after they were, so I don't think they would have known each other, but here's the interesting part."

"I'm all ears," Kelly said.

"One article I read said that the rumor was that Jessica had been dismissed from the cooking school because she had not personally prepared the food she was saying was hers. In other words, she cheated. Naturally, the people the article interviewed declined to give their names. They were probably afraid of getting sued for slander."

"Couldn't the newspaper be sued for libel for printing something like that?" Kelly asked.

51

"Probably not worth the effort. Their disclaimer that it was a rumor would probably suffice, since they were very clear that it was nothing more than a rumor. Plus, lawsuits are costly, so she probably just hoped no one would read the article," Mike said.

"She seems to have a background of not playing by the rules. Here's what Paul told me about her." Kelly recounted the conversation.

"That's all very interesting, but it doesn't mean she's the one who murdered Chef Jessup, although there does seem to be a history of animosity between the two women."

"But Mike, if Jessica did it, why would she come to the kitchen and ask to talk to Chef Jessup? She'd already know that the chef was dead."

"Kelly, never forget how devious criminal minds are. To you and me, that would make perfect sense. To someone who's committed murder, it might seem to be the perfect reason to ask to talk to someone and act like the person was still very much alive. Maybe she was hoping that by asking, people would never think she had anything to do with it."

"I suppose," Kelly said slowly, "although it seems like a strange thing to do."

"Not really. Let's say for the sake of argument that she did it. By asking to speak with the chef, she's more or less telling people that she couldn't have done it, because she wouldn't ask to speak with someone who was already dead."

"That's really weird. And if she did it, asking to have the chef come out of the kitchen for kudos would only add to the believability that she had nothing to do with or knew about the murder."

"Good deduction, Kelly." Mike stood up. "Now if you'll excuse me for a few minutes, I really do need to answer a couple of emails I've received from the sheriff's station back home. Take a break and we'll get to the diary in a few minutes."

CHAPTER ELEVEN

"This diary is a gold mine, Mike." Kelly said as she peered over the top of her reading glasses. "I'm so glad it came up in the conversation. I've bookmarked several pages, and I think we have some viable people of interest. First, I'll address the ones you've talked about. She goes into a little more detail on them."

"I'm going to lie down on the bed while you're talking, Kelly, and I promise you have my full attention. I will not go to sleep while you're talking."

"Considering the chief asked you to handle the case, not me, you better not. Here's what she wrote about her ex-husband and I quote, 'Ryan just won't give it up. He calls and texts me constantly threatening to do something terrible to me if I don't close the restaurant. As if. Who does he think he is? I built the restaurant, and if it turned out to be more popular than his, so be it. Guess he thinks those threats of physical abuse will make me close it. Fat chance. I made a vow when I left him that I would never again put myself in a situation where I could be abused, emotionally or physically, so closing the restaurant is not an option. If he intends to do something to me or the restaurant, bring it on.'"

"Hmmm, she says that he's been threatening her. When was that written?"

"She doesn't specifically have dates, but I think it was written about three weeks ago."

"I would definitely put him on the list of persons of interest. Who's next?"

"Daniel Moore, the chef from San Francisco. It's rather apparent that Chef Jessup didn't like him. She specifically says, 'Dan hasn't changed a bit. He's still believes women are secondary to men. In his latest phone call, he told me that I had no business having the special recipes of James Beard. He said that everyone knew that men made the best chefs, and my success was a fluke. For the first time he really threatened me by writing that if I didn't give him the recipes, I'd be sorry. Sorry how? I mean what can he do to me? I wrote him back and told him that I considered the matter closed, because I would never give him the recipes, and if he ever called me or tried to get in touch with me, I would contact my lawyer and get a restraining order against him."

"That seems like a definite threat, and it sounds like it's exactly what Chef Jessup took it for. Poor woman. Looks like there were a few people who weren't happy about her success," Mike said. "How much more, Kelly? I'm really struggling here. Tell me you're almost at the end. My body is crying for sleep."

"Tell your body it's in luck. She makes several references to Jessica, mainly about how much she doesn't like her, and she wishes she'd just move on to other things. I have one more definite person of interest to tell you about, and then you can give in to the demands of your body."

"Good, because I'm really ready to wrap this up for tonight," Mike said as he adjusted his pillow.

"Mike, this one is just plain weird, at least in my opinion."

"I'm waiting."

"She says she's been getting letters at the restaurant from a man named Alex Taylor, and that there's something off with him. And I quote, 'This guy is a loose cannon. He says he's been to the restaurant, and I have no business saying that the food is cooked in the manner of James Beard. He says that the spirits have told him that he's the reincarnation of James Beard, and he would never prepare the dishes the way I do. He's asked me to get rid of any references to Beard.' She goes on to say that the man has threatened to sue her and when he signs his letters, he signs them Alex Taylor aka James Beard. He says he's in the process of having his name legally changed to James Beard, and when that happens he will begin his lawsuit. She said he's threatened her with bodily harm if she doesn't do what he asks, and he also says he told her that her days were numbered. What do you think about that, Mike?"

"I think the world is full of wackos, that's what I think. I also think we've done as much as we can do for tonight and our bodies are craving sleep, at least mine is. I'm done. It's lights out time for me. See you in the morning. Love you."

Kelly set the diary on the nightstand and removed her glasses. "I'll turn off the light, but as much as my mind is whirling, I think it's going to be a while before I'm off to dreamland. Loves."

CHAPTER TWELVE

"Wake up, Kelly, I've brought you some coffee and bagels." Mike said as he gently shook her by the shoulder. "Thought you could use a little caffeine and something to eat before we get started. I saw Dakota when I was going to the restaurant and asked her about the guest list. She said she'd make a copy of the one she used to check people in for the James Beard dinner, so it will also have the no shows on it. She handed it to me when I walked out of the restaurant. I think we need to compare it to our people of interest list and see what shows up."

Kelly rubbed the sleep from her eyes and sat up. "Thanks for the coffee, Mike. I really had trouble getting to sleep last night, and I'm tired. This should definitely help. I'm going to take a quick shower and hope that will wake me up. Back in a minute."

Ten minutes later she walked back in the room, dressed and holding out her empty cup of coffee. "Mike, if you love me, you'll get me another one of these. Think one more is needed before my brain can kick into gear."

"No problem. Here's the list." He handed her the sheet of paper that Dakota had given him. "We definitely have some matchups. See what you think. Back in a few minutes, and don't worry about Rebel. I walked him while you were asleep."

"Thanks," she said as she sat down at the desk with the list in front of her.

I don't know what good this is going to do, but I see that Jessica and Alex both stayed here and came to the dinner last night. It looks like Daniel Moore cancelled, and there's no reservation for Chef Jessup's ex-husband, Ryan Stevenson.

She was looking at the list to see if she'd missed something when she heard Mike's voice at the door saying, "Kelly, it's me. Open the door. I can't open it with both of my hands holding cups of coffee."

"Will do." She walked over to the door and reached down to stroke Rebel as he followed Mike into the room. Accepting the coffee from Mike, she straightened up. "I looked at the list and it's interesting. Two of the people mentioned in Chef Jessup's diary stayed here last night. Maybe we can find something out from them if they're still here. I need to take you to the police station and get your car. How do you want to handle this?"

"First of all, I'd like to find out where Chef Moore and Chef Stevenson were late yesterday morning. If they were at their restaurants, that would pretty much rule them out. I think it's interesting that Chef Moore made a reservation, and then cancelled it. However, that doesn't mean he didn't do it. It just means he cancelled his reservation. Could have been a ploy to take suspicion away from him. And the fact that Chef Stevenson didn't make a reservation doesn't mean much either. Portland isn't that far from here."

"How do you plan to find out where Chef Stevenson was when Sam was killed?" she asked.

"I think I'll drive over to Portland and see if I can get any information on his whereabouts last night. I looked on the computer, and it stated that his restaurant serves lunch on Saturdays. What concerns me is that we're only about an hour and a half from Portland, and he easily could have driven over here, killed Samantha, and gone back. However, since the murder occurred sometime in the late morning, if he did go back to his restaurant, someone at the restaurant would have known if he wasn't there. It's been my experience that at that time of the day chefs are generally making sure everything is ready for the lunch and evening services, particularly when it's Friday night, which is usually one of their busiest nights."

"I agree. Do you know if the news of Chef Jessup's death has been released yet?"

"I haven't seen anything, so I'm hoping not. There's nothing in the local paper, which was in the rack downstairs. Chief Barnes said he wasn't going to release anything until he cleared it with me, because he didn't want to do anything that might hurt my investigation.

"He said that he'd told the coroner to just use the name 'Jane Doe' until he gave him the okay to use her real name. That's not an uncommon practice when law enforcement is trying to see what they can find out before the public is aware of it. Kind of an element of surprise thing. A lot of people call with false leads, and it takes time away from finding the real culprit."

Kelly set her coffee cup down. Her second one of the day was already down to the dregs. "Why would someone do that?"

"Believe me, I've wondered the same thing. It's kind of like why would you go to a funeral if you didn't know the person who died? But that doesn't stop folks from doing that. Sometimes, I'm really at a loss to understand why people do the things they do."

The room phone rang and Mike answered it. "Hi, Matt. Kelly and I were just trying to work out how we were going to go about getting the information we need to solve Chef Jessup's murder. What can I do for you?"

Mike was quiet as he listened to Matt, his eyes wide. "Seriously, Matt? Someone called and told you that if you didn't close the hotel, your family's lives would be in danger? Why would anyone do that?"

He held the phone to his ear, continuing to listen to Matt. Then Kelly heard him say, "You think it had something to do with that new hotel, the Rotunda? Why do you say that?"

He paused while Matt spoke. "I can understand that you give them competition," he said when Matt was done, "but surely they knew you'd be their competition when they built it."

Kelly stared at Mike with concern.

"Matt," he was saying, "I was getting ready to leave for Portland in a little while. I need to have Kelly take me to the police station, so I can get a car. If it's okay with you, I could meet with you in your office here at the hotel in about a half an hour and then head for Portland." He continued, "My concern is that the threat came on the heels of the murder. I want to hear everything about this new hotel, who runs it, what the background is on it, anything. See you in a little while." He set the receiver back into the handset with a click.

"Matt was threatened?" Kelly asked.

"Yes, his whole family was. You heard me. Maybe we're looking at the wrong motive. Maybe it had nothing to do with Chef Jessup, and she was just collateral damage. Maybe the murder happened so the Gearhart Hotel would get a lot of bad publicity. For all we know, maybe this Rotunda Hotel hoped they'd get reservations from people who were planning on coming to the coast but wouldn't want to stay at a hotel where a murder had taken place. Bad publicity can have that effect. I have no idea, but I'll know more after I've talked to Matt. Are you about ready to take me to the police station?"

Kelly picked up the car key. "Yes. While you're gone, I'll see what I can find out here at the hotel."

"I'll call you after my meeting with Matt. Let's go. I'm anxious to get this investigation started."

CHAPTER THIRTEEN

When Kelly returned to the hotel, she decided to take Rebel for a walk and then get some breakfast. She realized she'd never eaten dinner the night before, since her priority was making sure that the Beard dinner went seamlessly. The bagel Mike had brought her hadn't been enough, and she was still hungry.

When she walked downstairs to the restaurant the hostess said, "Please sit anywhere you like. Your server will be with you in a minute."

Kelly looked around at the crowded room and saw there was only one empty table. As soon as she sat down, her server brought her a pot of coffee and said he'd be back in a few minutes after she'd had time to look at the menu.

She was having trouble deciding between an omelet or the French toast. She scanned the menu looking for new things she could add to her breakfast menu, since it was important to her to update the breakfast menu from time to time with new items. Half of the customers who came to Kelly's Koffee Shop came for breakfast. She was almost finished when she heard a woman's voice ask, "May I share your table?"

She looked up and saw that it was Jessica Cartland, the food critic who had tried to get in the kitchen the evening before and after the dinner had asked to have Chef Jessup be acknowledged by the Beard dinner diners.

"I'm sorry to bother you, but I really am hungry, and there's nowhere else to sit. I'd really appreciate it," Jessica said with a smile.

"Certainly, sit down. When we spoke last night, I don't think I gave you my name. I'm Kelly Reynolds, and I was told that you are Jessica Cartland, the well-known food critic from The Oregonian."

Jessica had already pulled out a chair. "Yes, that's correct. I write a food column for the Oregonian, which includes reviews of local restaurants." Jessica sat down across the table from Kelly. She waved the server over and said, "I'll take a cup of coffee. Did you want a refill, Kelly?" she asked her.

"No, I'm fine right now, thanks. I heard the dinner guests were very pleased with everything last night. Will you be writing it up in your column? I've heard you do two a week. Would that be right?"

The server came over before Jessica had a chance to respond and took both of their orders. Kelly had opted for the crab and shrimp omelet, wondering why she'd never thought to put that on the menu at Kelly's Koffee Shop. Living in Oregon, crab and shrimp were always available, so it would be easy to prepare and serve. Jessica opted for the French toast.

"In answer to your question, yes, I do write two columns a week, and I intend to devote this week's columns to James Beard's food. Not only will I be highlighting the dinner that was held here last night, but I'm going to review several restaurants in Seaside and Cannon Beach that I understand specialize in the foods he liked."

Jessica poured two glasses of water from a carafe on the table and slid one across the table to Kelly. "I'm sorry, Kelly, but I'm not familiar with your name. Do you work with Chef Jessup?"

Interesting. If she is the murderer she seems oblivious to the fact that Chef Jessup has been murdered. Mike would probably say it could be a ploy, so I'd think she knows nothing about the murder.

"No. I never set eyes on her until yesterday. I own a coffee shop in Cedar Bay called Kelly's Koffee Shop, and for my birthday, my husband gave me the gift of coming here to the dinner and took it up a notch by asking the chef if I could be her sous-chef for the dinner. It was completely unexpected."

"What a thoughtful thing to do. Was it everything you hoped it would be? Did you learn a lot?" Jessica asked.

"Yes, I certainly did learn a lot. Her staff is devoted to her, and their expertise in the kitchen is amazing. It was quite an experience."

"What did you think of her?" Jessica asked.

Oh boy. I don't want to lie to her, but I don't want to tell her the truth about the chef's death. This is going to call for some real diplomacy.

"She's quite a person. As I said, her staff is devoted to her, and she's instructed them well. To see a team work together like they did says a lot for the person who trained them. It was something I'll never forget."

"Do you mind if I quote you in the article?" Jessica asked.

"Let me be frank, Jessica. I understand that you and Chef Jessup have not been on the best of terms in the past. If the article is going to be negative, no, I do not want to be quoted. If it's going to be positive, certainly you can use my name."

"You're absolutely right. Sam and I got off on the wrong foot a long time ago, and it's never improved over time. She still won't let me into her restaurant. I've had some health issues during the past year, actually some very serious health issues, but I won't bore you with the details. For the first time in my life, I came face to face with my own mortality and realized life is too short to spend it on petty things like fighting with a top chef.

"I made a vow to try and correct some of the mistakes I've made in my life. Guess it's kind of like an alcoholic when he becomes sober. I decided to make a list of all the people I've had problems with, and I'm trying to make amends with them. The rift between Sam and me is on that list. Her restaurant really is the best one in Portland, and it's because of her. She has a reputation in the industry that any chef would covet.

"The reason I came here this weekend was to apologize to her and tell her that the James Beard article I plan on writing was going to focus not only on him, but the legacy he left, Sam being the most famous of his adherents. Unfortunately, as you know, she wouldn't let me into the kitchen. I just hope when she reads the article she'll know that my admiration for what she's accomplished is genuine."

They paused while the waitress served the food. Kelly's omelet tempted her from the moment it was set on the table. When she cut into it she was pleased to find the consistency was just right. It was firm, but not too dry. The juicy shrimp and crab filling was generous without being overpowering.

"Thank you for being so honest, Jessica," Kelly said a few moments later. "I wish more people felt like you do but without having to go through a life-changing experience caused by health issues."

Jessica shrugged. "It certainly has given me a new perspective on life. When you have good health and feel like you have a lot of years ahead of you, atonement isn't very high on the list of things you need to accomplish before you meet St. Peter at the pearly gates."

"I'm going to change the subject," Kelly said. "This omelet is one of the best I've ever had. You might mention that James Beard loved seafood, and this omelet would certainly be a credit to him."

"Good idea. Just one more example of the ambiance of this hotel. I would like to ask a favor of you, Kelly. If you see Sam before I do, would you tell her that I really would like to bury the hatchet? Please ask her to read my upcoming piece on James Beard. I think she'll be pleased with what I'll be writing about her."

"I don't have any plans to see her, but if I do, I'll certainly relay the message," Kelly said as she stood up and put a twenty-dollar bill on the table to cover her breakfast. "My husband told me he'd be calling me about now, so I better go up to our room. I enjoyed talking to you, and I hope you stay in good health."

"Me too," Jessica said in an almost prayerful tone. "This has been the worst experience of my life, but it's also forced me to make some changes that have been a long time coming. Thanks for the conversation and who knows, I just might get to Cedar Bay someday and review Kelly's Koffee Shop."

I sincerely hope not, Kelly thought. *Obviously, the news about Chef Jessup's death hasn't been made public, and although everything I said to Jessica was true, it wasn't the whole truth, and given the way she's trying to lead her life now, I don't feel very good about it. She might not think too kindly of me if she ever finds out that I knew all along. Time to see if Mike's found out anything.*

CHAPTER FOURTEEN

Mike followed Dakota's directions to Matt's office and knocked on the door which was slightly ajar.

"Come in. The door's open," Matt said, and Mike stepped inside. "Have a seat. I know my office isn't very big, but when we refurbished the hotel, I didn't want to use any more space for my office than was absolutely necessary. Bare bones so to speak. In a hotel, every square foot that's wasted is money that could be made through guests, retail, or food."

"Makes sense," Mike said, "and good morning to you, or maybe I shouldn't use that phrase given the threat you received. Why don't you tell me about it?"

"Sheriff, it was really strange, and I think it has something to do with Chef Jessup's murder. The call came from an unidentified man. His voice was kind of muffled, and I remember thinking at the time that he might be holding a handkerchief or something over his phone to change the sound of his voice."

Mike took out his notebook and a pen. "You're probably right. That's not an uncommon practice for people who don't want to be recognized. Go on."

"He said, and I quote, because I'll never forget it. 'Matt, it's time to go public about Chef Jessup's murder. If you don't do it, your family will be very, very sorry.'"

"Where is your family right now?" Mike asked.

"They're at our home here in Gearhart. It's only a few blocks from the hotel. It's Saturday, so my daughter and son are at home. I called my wife and told her about the phone call. She freaked out. Nothing like this has ever happened to either one of us. I don't know what to do."

"Matt, you have security guards that work here at the hotel, don't you?"

"Yes, we have twenty-four-hour security. They don't wear uniforms, because we don't want to frighten the guests. This is a pretty sleepy little town and crime is rare, although the crime rate has been going up since the new hotel opened."

Mike was quiet for several long moments and then said, "First of all, can you have one of the people who works security here at the hotel go to your home and stay with your family when you're not there? I would think, since this seems to have something to do with the hotel, that the hotel would pay for it."

"Why didn't I think of that?" Matt said, slapping his forehead. "Yes, we have several people I could call, and I'm sure they could use the extra work. Excuse me while I make a call." He picked up the phone, pressed in a number, and said, "Bill, I have a little problem. I won't go into all of it now, but a threat has been made against my family. Any chance you could go over to my house, park on the street, and watch the house until I get home later this afternoon?"

He listened for a moment and then said, "Thanks. I'll call Julie and tell her to expect you in a few minutes. She's met you before, so that won't be a problem."

Matt looked across the desk at Mike. "Sorry, give me one more minute. I need to call my wife to let her know about Bill. That should ease her mind a bit." After the call, he looked at Mike and said, "You said first of all a few minutes ago. What's the next thing?"

"It seems to me there are two things going on here. The chef may have been murdered because of a personal matter, which is what I originally thought. However, after this threat, I think we need to explore who might want your hotel to get bad publicity. Maybe it had nothing to do with Chef Jessup. Can you think of anyone who would want to see the hotel have problems?"

Matt looked out the window at the golf course. It was an uncommonly beautiful day for this part of Oregon which was used to clouds, overcast skies, and rain. Today, however, the sun was shining and the course was filled with golf carts and golfers.

He looked back at Mike and said, "About six months ago a large hotel opened nearby called the Rotunda Hotel."

"Yes, I saw it when we got here yesterday. It seems to be much larger than yours. Kind of has a weird architectural style, as I recall. Has it affected your occupancy rate?"

"Not in the least, I'm happy to say. We have a clientele that often comes back year after year. People seem to like the casualness of this hotel. Besides the hotel being listed on the National Register of Historic Places, which is why some people want to stay here, we also have a number of guests who come to play on the oldest golf course west of the Mississippi.

"Additionally, we have events throughout the year that draw people, and of course, because of our expansive lawn and the setting, we host a number of weddings. People love the food in the Sand Trap Pub. And lastly, we're a dog-friendly hotel. I'd say about twenty percent of the people who come here bring their dogs."

"Okay, that takes care of your hotel. Now tell me about the Rotunda Hotel," Mike said.

"It's kind of a glitzy Las Vegas type hotel. Its theme is the United

States Capitol building. It has marble floors, European style furnishings, a fancy restaurant, and a state-of-the-art spa. I understand that some people from Las Vegas fronted the majority of the money to build it. From what I've heard, it's struggled to get guests. I've met the owner, or at least the partial owner, who runs it. His name is Bobby Lee.

"The talk originally was that he was going to get investors from mainland China to fund it, but for some reason, that didn't happen." Matt continued, "I've always wondered if the Chinese were smart enough to see that a hotel like that wouldn't appeal to visitors who wanted to come to the coast and stay in something that was Northwest in style and feel. The Rotunda is more like a Las Vegas strip hotel than an Oregon coast hotel. I don't think they did their homework when they built it."

"I'm thinking out loud, Matt, so bear with me. If I'm hearing you correctly, it sounds like you're saying that if your hotel got a lot of bad publicity or was closed, there's a good chance that the people who would have stayed here might stay at the Rotunda Hotel. Would that be about right?"

Matt took a moment to think about it and then said, "I suppose there could be some spillover, but the people who stay here are not the type of people you'd find at a Las Vegas style hotel. I can count on one finger the number of times a guest has ever asked if we have a spa. If you're thinking that could be a motive for the chef's murder, I'd have to say I think it's a longshot."

"Let's go at this another way," Mike said. "You just told me that Las Vegas people put the majority of the money up so the hotel could be built. Since I doubt they did it out of the goodness of their hearts, this guy Lee would have to pay the money back at some point. If his hotel is not doing well, I would think it would be hard to pay them back. Maybe in some twisted way, he's behind this, thinking problems here at your hotel would result in more guests at his hotel. Does that make any sense to you?"

"I think it's a real longshot. I can't say that I feel like I know him, although I've been around him a number of times at different city functions. He's just kind of cold. I was hoping originally that the two hotels might do some joint advertising and things of that nature. Attracting more visitors to the area is good business for everyone. I broached the subject with him once, and he said absolutely not. Something to the effect that people who stayed at his hotel would feel that staying at our hotel was a real step down for them. After that comment, I haven't had much to do with him.

"He got married a few months ago to a real looker who is quite a few years younger than he is. Talk on the street is that she's pretty bored living in Gearhart, not that that has anything to do with a murder or a threat."

"Probably not, but sometimes I find connections between things that are really far apart. I'll keep it in the back of my mind."

"Mike, when do you think the chief is going to release news of Chef Jessup's death? I want to be prepared, because I'm sure the press will come around looking for a story."

"I have no idea. When I spoke to Chief Barnes last night, his focus was on his son. He said once they knew what they were dealing with, he'd give a statement to the press regarding her death, but he didn't want to do it until he could give his full attention to it. The fact we've heard nothing tells me that he's still at the hospital or even in Portland. He told me he'd call when he knew something. Poor guy."

"I've known Kyle and his family for years. It's a really close family. No parent should have to go through something like that."

"Matt, let's take a moment to talk about the threat you received. It's been my experience they're usually nothing more than idle words. However, I'd always rather err on the side of caution, so I tend to take them seriously. Keep your doors locked, try and keep the kids occupied inside the house, and if you have a gun, I'd advise you to keep it near you. Here's my cell phone number." Mike pulled out his business card and handed it to Matt. "Since the chief is pretty much out of commission, feel free to call me if you notice anything unusual."

"I'm trying to put on a brave face, Mike, but I'm really concerned. I was thinking I wished I'd gotten the dog the kids wanted. We recently had a chance to get a boxer puppy, and I said no. Thought with two young kids in the house, the one thing we didn't need to deal with was the demands of a puppy. They're a lot of work. My wife's a teacher and puts in a lot of long hours. Our children are both in school now, and with my erratic hours, it seemed like too much. Now I'm regretting that decision."

Mike was quiet for a few moments and then he said, "Matt, this is going to sound pretty bizarre, but I think I can help you with that."

"You're going to get me a puppy?" Matt asked, laughing for the first time that day.

"No. My wife and I have an older boxer dog who's really a guard dog. He was a drug dog for law enforcement, but his handler died, and his wife had to get rid of him when the family moved. My wife took him in, and he's still the best guard dog I've ever been around. Matter of fact, he's saved her life a couple of times."

"That's all well and good, but I fail to see what you having a guard dog at home has to do with my present situation."

"I don't believe in coincidences. Guess there was a reason my wife and I brought Rebel with us on this trip. He's upstairs in our room right now. I think it would be a good idea if my wife took him over to your house, and you keep him until this situation is taken care of. Trust me, if Rebel's there, nothing is going to happen to your wife and kids."

"Mike, that sounds like the answer to my unasked prayer right now. One question. Will Rebel be okay around the children, because they'll probably pester him to death?" Matt said.

"Yes. We've always thought of him as a gentle giant. He loves children. Why don't you call your wife back and tell her that my wife,

Kelly, will bring him over to your house in a little while? I was going to call her when I was on the road to Portland, but since I've been delayed, she's probably in the room waiting for my call right now. Let me have your address and directions. Kelly and Rebel will take it from there."

"Do you one better, Mike. Since your wife's probably not too familiar with the streets in Gearhart, I'll print out a map for her."

A few minutes later he handed Mike the map and said, "I can't thank you enough for doing this. I know there's still a murderer on the loose, but at least I feel I'm doing everything I can for my family."

"Let's just say, Matt, after you spend a little time with Rebel, you'll probably be getting your kids a present, a boxer pup." He grinned as he stood up. "Talk to you when I know something," he said as he left Matt's office.

CHAPTER FIFTEEN

When Mike opened the door to the hotel room Kelly did a doubletake from her seat in front of the dressing table. "I'm surprised to see you," she said, "I thought you were on your way to Portland. I was waiting for you to call me."

"I was planning to, but the meeting with Matt went a little longer than I thought it would. I know you won't mind, but I took the liberty of volunteering Rebel's services."

Kelly set her hairbrush down. "I think I'm missing something here, Mike. What does Rebel have to do with Matt?"

He told her about his meeting with Matt, his offer, and ended by saying, "Sorry, Kelly. Not only did I offer Rebel's services, I told Matt you would take Rebel over to his house this morning. He was calling his wife when I left his office, so I'm sure the children are already excited. Here's a map with directions on how to get to his house. I understand it's really nearby."

"I'm fine with that, Mike, and Rebel will love all the extra attention. You know how much he loves children. I can only imagine how scared Matt must be about this. I'm glad we can help by letting him keep Rebel. Hopefully, we can get this thing solved pretty soon."

"Thanks, Kelly. I've got another favor to ask of you."

"Shoot, Sheriff. It's not as if I have a lot on my agenda at the moment. What is it?"

"I told you what Matt said about the new hotel, the Rotunda. While I'm in Portland this afternoon I'd like you to go over there, maybe have lunch, and get a spa treatment. Sort of nose around and see if you can find out anything of interest."

"Will do, and it's a great way for me to justify getting a massage. Is there anything in particular you want me to look for?"

"No. I'm just trying to cover all the bases, and that happens to be one of them. If nothing else, you can have a gourmet lunch and a great spa treatment. I'm going to take Rebel out for a quick walk before you take him over to Matt's house. Back in a few."

Kelly walked over to the phone in the room and asked the operator if she could have the number for the Rotunda Spa. When Mike and Rebel returned from their walk, she was ready to go to Matt's home. "I have an appointment for a massage at the spa at 1:30 this afternoon. I should be back here around 3:00. When do you think you'll be back from Portland?"

Mike screwed up his face while he thought for a moment. "Probably a little later than that. Depends on what I find out. It's about a three hour round trip, plus time for lunch and whatever time I need to talk to people. Good luck, and Kelly, I know how much you love this big guy," Mike said petting Rebel. "I appreciate your sacrifice, but I think it's for a good cause. I know it made Matt feel a lot better." He handed the leash to Kelly.

"Happy to be of service. Drive safely. Loves."

*****

When Mike had left, Kelly spoke to Rebel. "Okay, Mr. Awesome, guess it's time for me to take you to meet some people you're going to help. You shouldn't be there too long. Let's go." She tugged on his leash, and they walked down the stairs and out to the car.

A few minutes later she pulled up in front of a large one-story home with grey shake siding and white trim. Spruce trees surrounded the rear of the house and brightly colored flowers spilled out of hanging baskets on the porch overhang. A perfectly-trimmed hedge separated the front lawn from the driveway. It was obvious the house was well maintained.

She'd just opened the back door of the car for Rebel when the front door of the house burst open, and a tall blond woman with her hair pulled back in a ponytail walked out of the house holding the hands of a little boy and a little girl.

"Hi," she said. "I'm Julie Parker, and you must be Kelly Reynolds. Obviously, we've been looking for you. I assume this handsome boy is Rebel."

"I am, and he is," Kelly said.

"Mommy, can I pet him?" the little boy asked.

Julie looked down at her son. "No, Aiden, not until you've been properly introduced." She turned to Kelly. "These are my children, Aiden and Kayla. I must warn you, they're pretty excited about this. Why don't you two come in the house, and you can tell me what I need to do."

Kelly looked at the children and said, "Aiden, why don't you take the leash and walk Rebel into the house? Kayla, when they get in the house why don't you unhook Rebel's leash? That way he'll know that he has my permission for him to go with you."

The children walked Rebel up to the house and took him inside. Julie looked at Kelly and said, "You must have children. That was masterful. I wasn't quite sure how I was going to handle this, since both of the kids are so excited they can barely stand it. We may have some problems going on over at the hotel, but the silver lining is that Rebel's coming to stay with us for a few days. Thank you."

Kelly spent the next half hour instructing the children on the best way to handle Rebel. She reminded them that sometimes dogs need a time out and that Rebel was an older dog and needed a morning nap and an afternoon nap.

"Julie, Aiden, Kayla, it was nice meeting you," she said as she prepared to leave. "Enjoy Rebel, and I can see he's going to be well taken care of. Rebel, you take care of them," Kelly said, noticing that Rebel was licking the children's hands while they both petted him.

Julie walked Kelly into the hallway. "Kelly, thank you. I feel so much better now. Between Rebel and Bill, he's the one over there sitting in the car, we're going to be fine. Hopefully, this will be over pretty soon."

Kelly waited until they were out of earshot of the children before speaking. "Julie, I'm sure none of these things will happen, but there are a couple of things you should know. If Rebel growls, there's a reason for it. If you feel something's not right, give him the command, 'On Guard.' If an intruder does get in the house, give him the command, 'Attack.'

"Once he's subdued the person, give him the command, 'Stand Down.' He'll put his full weight on the person until someone comes to help. When law enforcement arrives, and they get ready to put handcuffs on the person or whatever, give him the command, 'That's All.' He's been well trained and knows what to do if you say any of those things. You and the children are his people now, so he'll do everything he can to protect you. I speak from experience, he's very good at protecting his person, or in this case, persons."

Julie opened the front door. "We'll be fine. I'm just sorry we have to take him from you, but I certainly appreciate it," she said.

When Kelly was gone, Julie turned and walked back into the house. As she was opening her car door, Kelly heard Kayla say, "Mommy, Aiden says Rebel gets to sleep in his room tonight. That's not fair. I want him in my room."

Yeah, Kelly thought, *this will make up for all the times Lady and Skyy got some attention. For now, he really is the top dog.*

CHAPTER SIXTEEN

Mike looked at his watch as he walked out of the parking structure near Pioneer Square in Portland. It was just after 1:00, and he thought it should be fairly slow at the restaurant at that time of day on a Saturday. He looked around and saw the oblong white sign with "Pioneer Grill" spelled out in red letters on a red brick building, just off the square. A valet stand was in front of it.

When he entered the restaurant, he understood why it had become so popular. It was an old-fashioned clubby type of restaurant, like the ones from the 1950's and 1960's. It was the kind of restaurant that made you want to stay in it and not venture out into the rain. Tall glass mid-century block dividers with wave motifs separated the booths and allowed for privacy.

Since the Pioneer Grill was in the downtown district of Portland with a number of high-end hotels nearby, Mike was certain that a large part of its clientele must come from business people in town for a few days of meetings. A restaurant that had this ambiance and was known for fine dining would be a perfect place to meet.

After he'd entered, he looked around and was amazed at the number of people who were in the restaurant. When he approached the hostess stand, he noticed that the long ornate bar on one side of the restaurant was completely filled. "I'd like a table for one. I don't have a reservation," Mike said.

"Please, follow me." The attractive red-haired hostess with the greenest eyes he'd ever seen picked up a menu and led him through the restaurant to a small table in the back. "Your server today is Andrew. He'll be with you shortly. May I get you something to drink?"

"Yes, I'd like a Common Urban Farmhouse Ale," Mike said.

"I'll take care of that, sir. Enjoy your meal," she said as she turned his order into the bar and walked back to the hostess stand.

A moment later a young man appeared at the end of the table. "Hello. My name is Andrew. Here is your beer. Are you ready to order or would you like to look at the menu for a few more minutes?" he asked.

"Andrew, what's your favorite thing on the menu?" Mike asked. "I'm having trouble choosing, and I'm always happy to go on recommendations."

"I'm kind of a simple guy, but Chef Stevenson makes a mean meat loaf for the dinner service. The next day it's on the menu as a meat loaf sandwich. It comes with home fries and pickles. It's my favorite."

"Sounds good to me. That's what I'd like. Thanks, Andrew."

"Should only be a few minutes," the young man said as he walked over to a computer that was mounted on the wall and entered Mike's order. A few minutes later he returned with a large square plate and the biggest sandwich Mike had ever seen.

"Andrew, you didn't tell me it was for two people," Mike said with a laugh. "I'm not sure I'll even be able to lift it, much less eat it, but it does look delicious."

Andrew grinned, revealing chunky metal braces on his teeth. "Trust me, sir, once you start, you'll finish it. Everyone does, even after they say something like what you just said."

"Is this the chef's own invention?" Mike asked.

"As I understand it, yes. I believe a few of the items on the menu are ones he and his ex-wife came up with and even after she left the restaurant, they were so popular he kept them on. The rest of the items are his own invention. I've never understood why The Pioneer Grill hasn't gotten the best restaurant in Portland designation. Kind of adds insult to injury that his ex-wife's restaurant, The Pampered Hamburger, did. I know he wishes she'd just close it and go away."

"I'm from out of town, but I read excellent restaurant reviews on both of them. From what I'm seeing today, and Saturday lunches are usually a slow time, seems like plenty of people like it here. What makes you say the chef wants his ex-wife to close her restaurant and leave?"

"He doesn't like to be in competition with her. I've never met her, but a lot of people say she's a real perfectionist, and it was always tense when the two of them were in the kitchen together. He's low key, and I guess she's not. That's about all I know. Anyway, as far as how busy it is, it's always this way. You should have seen it yesterday. It was crazy. Good thing Chef Stevenson can keep his cool when we're in the weeds, because for some reason, yesterday at lunch was a prime example."

"Sorry, Andrew, you must be speaking restaurant lingo. I don't know what you mean."

"No problem. It just means too many orders are coming in, and it's really hard to get them out on time. Yesterday was like that. I rotate weeks between the lunch shift and the dinner shift. Today's my last day for lunch shifts. Tomorrow I'll switch to nights for a week then back again."

"So, the chef was calm and cool when all those orders came in?" Mike asked, thinking that if the chef was in the restaurant for lunch yesterday, there was no way he could have gone to Gearhart and murdered Chef Jessup.

"Yeah, the guy's amazing. He was actually plating the food and doing all kinds of other things to make sure things went smoothly. I've worked in a couple of other restaurants, but Chef Stevenson makes the other chefs in town look like wannabes by comparison."

"I'm sure the chef admires your loyalty, Andrew. Thanks for taking the time to talk to me, since it's so busy."

"You're right. I'm sure a couple of other orders are up. Enjoy your meal."

Interesting. Guess we can cross Chef Stevenson off of the people of interest list. Andrew obviously thinks highly of him. He had no reason to lie about the chef being in the kitchen during the lunch hour yesterday, plus the guy can make one heck of a meat loaf sandwich. The last reason for taking him off the possible suspects list is probably not according to law enforcement procedures, but I can't put anyone on a persons of interest list who can cook like that.

CHAPTER SEVENTEEN

When they'd first arrived in Gearhart, Kelly had been so busy looking for the hotel where they'd be staying, she hadn't noticed the Rotunda Hotel. Now she wondered how anyone could miss it. The words, *what was someone thinking when they built that monstrosity?* sprang to her mind when she drove up to the hotel and spa that resembled the Capitol in Washington, D.C. It was completely white with evenly spaced Doric columns.

Above the white columns was a frieze like the one seen on the U.S. Capitol. Kelly remembered how awestruck she'd been upon seeing the capitol when she'd been a chaperon and accompanied her daughter's high school class on their annual trip to Washington, D.C. Looking at the building in front of her, she couldn't believe anyone would build a hotel that looked like the capitol on the Oregon Coast, and hope to fill it with hotel and spa guests.

She pulled up under the Doric-columned parking entrance where her door was immediately opened by a young valet dressed in the Revolutionary style of Paul Revere.

Stranger and stranger, she thought as she climbed out of her car and thanked him. "Welcome to the Rotunda Hotel," he said.

A similarly dressed doorman opened the main hotel entrance for her and repeated the words as she entered the hotel. When she walked into the large entry hall she froze in shock. Above her was a dome, similar to the rotunda on the Capitol, and The Frieze of American History, a painted panorama depicting significant events in American history, outlined the top of the dome.

The United States Capitol on a Pacific Ocean bluff? Never had anything in her travels seemed so out of place. And to dress the staff in American Revolutionary clothing. The theme had been carried out to include the people manning the reservation desk and even the concierge. The women wore outfits that bore a resemblance to what she supposed Betsy Ross had dressed like and the men wore the Paul Revere styles. A large marble sign painted in red, white, and blue pointed the way to the Freedom Restaurant.

"Hi," Kelly said to the hostess when she had taken it all in. "One for lunch, please."

"Would you prefer to sit inside or outside?" the pretty young hostess asked.

"Inside will be fine."

The young woman led her to a booth which looked out on a flower-filled courtyard. There were several tables and booths occupied near hers, but the rest of the restaurant was unoccupied. The woman handed her a menu. "Thanks for coming to the Freedom Restaurant. Your waiter will be with you shortly."

A few minutes later a young waiter with the name tag, Zack, brought her a bottle of sparkling water and asked if she'd like anything else to drink while she was making her decision. "Yes, I'd like a glass of iced tea and a few more minutes to look over the menu. Is there anything you specifically recommend?" she asked.

"No, because everything is wonderful. We have one of the top chefs on the West Coast, and I consider him to be a genius." Zack's enthusiasm was evident in his voice.

"Sounds to me like you want to be a chef, Zack. Would I be

right?" Kelly asked.

"Yes, I'm staging here in the evenings. You know, a trainee to the chef. In return I work the lunch shift. I've learned so much. The chef says I have talent, and he's asked management if he can hire me. I'm keeping my fingers crossed. To have a chance to work for a top restaurant and actually have an experienced chef train me, and for money, would be like my dream come true."

"Well, if it helps, I'll keep my fingers crossed as well."

Zack was distracted momentarily. "Excuse me, I see that Amanda Lee, the owner's wife, just came in. I need to get her wine. I'll be back in a few minutes."

Kelly glanced at the booth next to her where the hostess had seated two women. The booth was quite close to where she was sitting, and she couldn't help but hear Zack say to one of the women, "Mrs. Lee, it's good to see you. Here's a glass of your favorite pinot noir, Mimi's Mind from the Lingua Franca Winery. The bartender poured it as soon as he saw you walk in."

He turned to the other woman and said, "May I get you something to drink while you're looking at the menu?"

"Yes, I'll have the same as Mrs. Lee."

"Certainly, I'll be right back with it."

A moment later he returned with the wine and said, "Have you decided on anything, or would you like a few more minutes to look at the menu?"

Mrs. Lee said, "I'll have the usual, a shrimp Louie salad, with the dressing on the side."

Zack turned to her companion. "And you, ma'am, have you decided on anything?"

"Yes, I'd like the scallop pasta with alfredo sauce. That sounds delicious."

"Good choice, ma'am. It's one of my favorites. Enjoy the view, and I'll return in a few minutes. Mrs. Lee, would you care for another glass of wine?"

"Yes, I would," she said as she finished the first glass of wine Zack had brought her less than two minutes earlier.

He turned away from their booth and stopped at Kelly's on his way to the bar to get Mrs. Lee's wine, menus tucked under his arm. "Have you made your decision?" he asked.

"Yes. I couldn't help but overhear the woman at the other booth order scallop pasta with alfredo sauce. I'd like that."

"As I told her, good choice."

Kelly looked at the menu and jotted down some notes of things she could serve at Kelly's Koffee Shop. She wasn't eavesdropping, but she couldn't help but overhear the conversation between Amanda Lee and the other woman as it drifted her way.

"Nikki, I was really surprised when Bobby told me that you and Alex were coming to Gearhart, but that you weren't going to stay here at the Rotunda. I know how much he enjoys having his nephew here. Then he said something about that funky little hotel down the road doing a James Beard dinner, and that you and Alex had reservations for it. What's that all about?" Amanda Lee asked the woman sitting across from her as she took a drink of wine from the glass Zack had set in front of her.

"You know Alex. He just keeps going deeper and deeper into this James Beard thing." Kelly saw Nikki roll her eyes. "I mean, at first I didn't think much of it because he'd always liked to cook. Then he got a bunch of video tapes of Beard's old cooking shows. That's when he really became obsessed by Beard. Honestly, I don't know how this is going to end. He has this thing that no chef should say they cook in the style of James Beard. It's really becoming an embarrassment."

"Why would he say something like that? A lot of chefs cook like well-known chefs. Look at all the chefs who say they cook in the style of Julia Child."

"Yeah, but none of them say they are the reincarnation of Julia Child."

Amanda put her glass down and looked at Nikki, open-mouthed. "Seriously? Are you telling me Alex thinks he's James Beard?"

Nikki put her head in her hands for a moment and then looked up. "Yeah, believe it or not, Alex thinks, no believes, really believes that he's the reincarnation of James Beard. Even worse, he's making these noises that people who try to copy James Beard shouldn't be allowed to live. I mean, it's surreal. I've suggested he see a psychiatrist, but he asks me what for? He says the psychiatrist would recognize that he is the reincarnation of James Beard. He can discuss it quite rationally. I actually fear he's slipped over the edge."

Their conversation was interrupted by Zack, as he served them lunch, and then brought Kelly her scallop pasta. Amanda and Nikki were quiet for a few moments, enjoying their meal.

"Amanda, this is your husband's hotel. Do me a favor and tell him that I think the meals here at the Freedom rival any I've had at other top-notch restaurants."

"I'll tell him. Looking at the lack of people here today, he can probably use a little good news."

"How's the room occupancy rate going? I know he was concerned about that the last time I saw him."

"Not good at all. I think what really frustrates him is that the hotel down the road, The Gearhart, is always full, and I don't know why. Our hotel has better food, a spa, and lavish guestrooms. I don't know if I ever told you, but he borrowed a lot of money from some of his brother's friends in Las Vegas, and his first payment is due pretty soon. It's getting to be crunch time around here."

Nikki took several bites of her pasta dish and then raised her napkin to her mouth before continuing to speak. "Amanda, it's none of my business, but one time you mentioned that if Bobby didn't make a go of it, you might not be around to see the results. Still thinking that way?"

"Yeah. I decided a long time ago life's too short to spend it with losers. I really thought Bobby was going to make it big. I was wrong. Should have listened to my intuition and invested my time in his brother. At least he's got the real deal going on over in Vegas."

"What's that?"

"He's the main person that put together that hotel in Vegas that caters to the Chinese. His friends hired him to run the hotel in Vegas because he's Chinese and knows what the Chinese gamblers want in a hotel. His friends are the ones who built it. I mean everybody knows what big gamblers the Chinese are, and from what Bobby tells me, the hotel in Vegas is standing room only all year long. If I'd gone with Bobby's brother I'd be the wife of some Chinese bigwig instead of the wife of an owner of a hotel that will probably have to close before its first anniversary."

"Well, I guess neither one of us is in a real good place at the moment, are we?" Nikki asked.

"No," Amanda said, "but I've learned there are ways to beat the boredom of this nothing town, if you know what I mean. And what I mean is my standing appointment for my daily massage. I don't want to be late, so go ahead and stay if you want. I'll talk to you later," she said standing up and walking down the hall towards the spa.

Well, this has certainly been interesting. Nikki must be Alex Taylor's wife; the Alex Taylor Chef Jessup wrote about in her diary. And what she said about him being the reincarnation of James Beard sure fits in. Wait until Mike hears about this. Kelly enjoyed the rest of her lunch in uninterrupted silence.

*****

"Zack, my compliments to the chef," Kelly said to the young waiter after she'd told him she'd pass on dessert. "The scallop pasta was wonderful. Tell me something. Did you say that was Mrs. Lee, the owner's wife, who was sitting in the booth next to me?"

"Sure was. She eats lunch here every day, and then she goes to the spa for a massage," he said, rolling his eyes. "She's actually pretty nice, but I hear she may be leaving Mr. Lee if things don't improve financially around here. I mean a woman who looks like her could probably have any man she wants, at least that's what I think."

"Hmmm. Seems like Mr. Lee would have enough on his plate just trying to make a go of this hotel without having marital problems."

"Don't think when he married her he thought there would be any problems. He's told everyone around this area that this hotel is the finest in the Northwest. Unfortunately, not many people have come to see if what he says is true. He married her while the hotel was being built and told everyone that it was his wedding present to her."

"So, reading between the lines," Kelly said, "it looks like Mrs. Lee was given a wedding present that pretty much nobody else wants now. I can see where that could be a problem."

"That's about it, and to tell you the truth, if this hotel doesn't make it, the chef has already told me he's looking around for another job and would like for me to go with him."

"I would think that would be a great opportunity for you," Kelly said. "Being as fine a chef as he is, I'm surprised that he wasn't asked to be the chef for the James Beard dinner last night at the Gearhart."

"I know I shouldn't tell you this. He applied, but he wasn't accepted. I don't know who chose Chef Jessup, but it's probably because she's considered the heir apparent in Oregon to James

Beard's way of cooking. Actually, it was probably a good thing our chef wasn't chosen. I guess Mr. Lee really hates the Gearhart Hotel and thinks if they weren't around, the Rotunda would be filled every night, and who knows? He might be right."

Kelly leaned back while Zack cleared her plate off the table. "I'm sure word of that has reached the management of the Gearhart Hotel, and I don't think they'd want to hire a chef who worked for a hotel that hated them. I imagine they'd worry about some type of deviousness taking place. I know I would."

"You're probably right. I heard that Chef Jessup cooked a heck of a dinner last night, and everyone was really pleased with it. I wish I could have afforded to go. She's got a fabulous reputation among the chefs, not to mention being the chef/owner of the most highly regarded restaurant in Portland, The Pampered Hamburger."

"Although I wasn't a guest at the event, several people who did attend have mentioned it was one of the best meals they've ever had."

That's the truth. I wasn't a guest there. I just helped get that meal on the tables.

"I've got to go," Zack said, "Looks like we have some more customers, and that's a good thing."

"I've really enjoyed talking to you, Zack, and wish you the best of luck. I'm sure you'll do well. Someday I hope to eat at a restaurant and see that you're the chef."

"If you see the name Zack Martin on the menu, please let the waiter know that you'd like to talk to me. And your name is?" he asked.

"My name is Kelly Reynolds, and if I do see your name on a menu, I'll definitely do that. Again, good luck. I'll get my check on the way out."

CHAPTER EIGHTEEN

When Kelly was leaving the restaurant, she asked the hostess for directions to the Sanctuary spa and followed them to a building set apart from the main hotel. It followed the architectural style of the hotel with a large rotunda-type dome over what appeared to be the reception area, according to the sign on the door.

She opened it and saw the spa receptionist sitting at a circular mahogany computer desk in the center of the room. The round walls of the room had shelving with various beauty and spa products displayed on them. The lighting was dimmed and she could detect the faint scent of sandalwood in the air. Soft music added to the ambiance, one of relaxation.

Kelly walked over to the desk and greeted the receptionist. "Hi, my name is Kelly Reynolds, and I have a 1:30 massage appointment. I know I'm a few minutes early."

The receptionist smiled and said, "Welcome to the Sanctuary. Let me locate your appointment." She tapped the keys of her sleek computer keyboard. A moment later she said, "Here it is. You're scheduled for a Rejuvenation Massage with Ramona. Please, follow me."

The woman led her down a hall and into a room with lockers, showers, and complementary beauty products. "You can put your things in locker number 503. The key is on a bracelet you can take with you to your treatment." She pointed to a closet and said, "You'll find a robe and slippers in there. When you've finished changing clothes, the Reflection room is through that door. There are candles if you feel like meditating. Ramona will meet you there when it's time for your appointment. It's a place to relax. See you later."

Kelly changed her clothes and opened the door leading to the unoccupied meditation room. Soft, soothing music played, and the smell of sandalwood incense was a little stronger in this room, where the décor was one of shades of pale white. A cascading waterfall was in one corner of the off-white room. Cream-colored chaise lounges filled the space and every table had pastel bouquets of fresh flowers in vases. The latest magazines had been tastefully arranged on tables. A long off-white credenza filled one wall with different types of cookies on a glass tray, and a large cut glass pitcher was filled with water, ice, and sliced cucumbers.

No wonder this is called the Reflection or Meditation room, Kelly thought. *I could spend hours in this oasis the spa has created. It's one of the most peaceful, well-appointed rooms I've ever been in. It's as cozy as a cloud.*

She poured herself a glass of the cucumber iced water and settled on one of the chaises, pulling a soft pale pink throw over her feet and legs. Kelly closed her eyes and relaxed, thinking of the events of the last twenty-four hours, and trying to make sense of them. The music washed over her, and she felt her heartbeat slow down.

"Mrs. Reynolds," a woman's voice said, bringing her back to the present, "I'm Ramona, your massage therapist. Please come with me."

Kelly followed her down a hall that had oil paintings of scenes from the 1800's, which seemed completely out of keeping with the New Age feel to the Reflection room. Her senses were jarred, and not in a particularly good way.

Ramona opened a door and motioned her inside. "You can hang your robe and spa locker bracelet on the peg here. Please lie face down under the sheet. I'll be back in a few minutes."

Kelly hung her robe and bracelet on the peg and got under the warm sheet. A few minutes later there was a knock on the door and Ramona said, "May I come in?"

"Yes, I'm under the sheet and the warmth of it feels wonderful," Kelly said.

"You'll feel even better once I put this light blanket over you. Is there anything I should know about you before I begin? Are you having any problems?" Ramona asked.

"No, I'm in good health, and I don't have any particular aches and pains other than those of aging."

"You're lucky," Ramona said. "You wouldn't believe the health problems I see." She began to lightly knead Kelly's upper back. Her hands were cool and firm.

"Have you been with the spa for long?" Kelly asked.

"I started working for Mr. Lee the day he opened the spa. Actually, he's been a client of mine for years. I used to work out of my home, and he was one of my first clients. He begged me come to work at the spa, and so I did. Although now I wonder if that was such a good idea," she said as she worked her way down Kelly's body.

Kelly felt knots in her body disappear that she didn't even know were there. Ramona's technique was methodical, yet at the same time soothing, and she understood why Bobby Lee had wanted her to work at his spa.

"Why do you say that?"

Ramona's voice was at odds with the heavenly music being piped through the invisible sound system. "Well, I probably shouldn't reveal this, but there are some things going on around here that I don't like. I just don't know if I should tell Mr. Lee about them," she said, her tone judgmental.

Kelly was burning with curiosity, but didn't want to seem to eager, so she said, "I can imagine you do see a lot working in a spa."

"You have no idea. Mr. Lee has enough problems on his mind without having to worry about his wife. I knew something like this would happen when he married her. I told him so," she sniffed.

"You're right. I have no idea. What kind of problems is he having?" Kelly asked innocently.

"Turn over, Mrs. Reynolds. I need to do your arms and legs." Kelly did as she was instructed, and Ramona continued, "Mr. Lee still comes to me twice a week for massages, and the last few weeks that man has been wound so tight, it's all I can do to get the kinks out. And then his wife…"

"What about his wife?" Kelly asked.

"Well, you didn't hear it from me," Ramona said, clearly warming to the subject, "But I can pretty much tell you why Mrs. Lee has a massage scheduled for 1:00 every day, and it's not to get the knots out of her body," she harrumphed.

She continued to knead Kelly's arms and legs. "Everybody on the staff of the spa knows what's going on in Andres' massage room when Mrs. Lee is in there."

"I'm sorry, Ramona, but I'm not following you. I understand Mrs. Lee has a standing massage appointment. What else would go on there?"

Ramona's hands stilled and she paused before whispering, "I'm a God-fearing woman. What goes on in that massage room is just not right for a married woman. Andres is giving a new meaning to the term Latin lover. And the worst part, from what I hear, is that he's also getting paid for that hour. And it's Mr. Lee's money. Think the word gigolo is a better term for Andres than masseur."

"Am I to understand that you think Mrs. Lee is being unfaithful to her husband?" Kelly asked innocently.

"That's exactly what I'm saying, and that's not all," she said, obviously agitated. "Mr. Lee has helped his nephew so much, and he just gets odder and odder. He always comes to me for a massage when he's in town. Matter of fact he was in here yesterday." She stopped talking while she poured warm oil on Kelly's legs.

"He's gone off the deep end, if you ask me," she resumed. "All he talks about now is how he's the reincarnation of James Beard. Guess he got fired from his job at that food company where he worked. He told me if he could just get rid of all the James Beard wannabes, he'd finally be recognized as the man. He was pretty angry about some of the chefs who cook in the style of Beard. He mentioned he was going to go to that Beard dinner at the Gearhart Hotel last night."

"Do you think he really believes he's the reincarnation of James Beard?" Kelly asked.

"Sure do. I also do massages for his wife when they come to town, and she's worried sick about him. Mrs. Taylor's really nice. She told me he slipped over the edge a few months ago, and she doesn't know what's going to happen to him. She told me she'd been to a doctor to see if she could get him committed to a mental institution, but the doctor said he's in a grey area since he's not dangerous to himself or others, and no judge would commit him.

"That's probably the reason there's so many nut cases out there on the streets. Guess they all fall into that grey area. I'd like to see them all in institutions, but I guess there aren't enough, and judges can't commit them. Seems like something's wrong with the system when that happens," she sniffed.

Kelly nodded as best she could. "I agree. What do you think he'll do now that he doesn't have a job?"

"Well, his wife told me that he wanted to be the chef here at the hotel restaurant and rename the restaurant The James Beard Restaurant. Fortunately, Mr. Lee told him no. I guess Alex wasn't very happy about it. Now, we've talked long enough. Close your eyes. I want you to just relax while I finish your massage."

Kelly followed Ramona's advice and spent the remaining time simply enjoying the way her body felt. Somewhat later, she realized she'd dozed off when Ramona said, "Mrs. Reynolds, please feel free to stay here for a few more minutes. I've enjoyed talking to you, and I hope if you return to the spa, you'll ask for me."

"Ramona, that was wonderful," Kelly murmured, trying to resist the temptation to keep her eyes closed and stay in the moment for longer, but she had work to do and was sure Mike would be interested in the information Ramona had just divulged to her. "And if I do return to the spa I definitely will ask for you. Thank you."

CHAPTER NINETEEN

A few minutes after Mike left the restaurant, he turned onto Highway 26 on his way back to Gearhart. He'd crossed one suspect off the persons of interest list, Ryan Stevenson, Chef Jessup's ex-husband, and still had several to go. Jessica Cartland, Alex Taylor, and Bobby Lee, were all in Gearhart, so he decided to see what Kelly had come up with before he pursued those avenues. There was one other person of interest from Chef Jessup's diary that needed to be taken care of, Daniel Moore, the chef from San Francisco.

Mike was mulling over whether he should take a quick trip to San Francisco when he remembered that he'd met the San Francisco Chief of Police at the Baker to Las Vegas Challenge Cup Relay Race for law enforcement personnel. The team from his county, Beaver, Oregon, had placed third, losing by just five minutes to the San Francisco team.

Mike's recollection of it was vivid. The race is an annual event run by relay teams composed of nearly 8,000 law enforcement personnel from around the world. It starts in Baker, California and ends at the Hilton Hotel in Las Vegas, a distance of slightly more than one hundred miles.

He pulled over to the side of the highway, took his phone out of his pocket and brought up Chief Morgan's phone number. He pulled back on the highway, and using the Bluetooth in his borrowed police vehicle, called the chief.

"Chief Morgan here. What can I do for you?" The same gruff voice Mike remembered answered the call.

"Chief it's Mike Reynolds, Sheriff Mike Reynolds from Beaver County, Oregon. We met at the Baker to Vegas race last year. I'm still smarting over that last-minute push during the final stage when your team beat ours."

The chief's hearty laugh boomed down the line. "Good to hear your voice, Mike, and I have to tell you that the morale of the police department was at an all-time high when we got back to the department after the race. Are you going to be involved in it this year?"

"We haven't decided yet." Mike chuckled. "Maybe we should just rest on our third-place laurels. Might do our morale some real damage if our guys finished lower than last year. Think we'll keep those bragging rights, but we're keeping our options open," he said.

"Probably a good idea. I might do the same, but I doubt you called just to check and see if we were going to run the race this year." The chief's tone turned businesslike.

"Spoken like a true cop. You're absolutely right. I have a favor to ask of you. There's a well-known chef in San Francisco by the name of Daniel Moore. He owns a restaurant called Beard's Bistro. Here's why I'm calling, and the details about the favor I'd like to ask."

Mike spent the next ten minutes telling the chief about Chef Jessup's murder, the diary, and the possible suspects. When he was finished he said, "I'd really consider it a favor if you'd have someone check to see if Chef Moore was at his restaurant yesterday. If he was, I can cross him off my suspect list. If not, I'll have to do some more digging to find out just where he was around the time when Samantha Jessup was killed."

"Not a problem, Mike. Think you got lucky with this one, because the odds are about one hundred to nothing that you can cross him off the list, but I'll double check. Thing is, one of my men is getting married in a couple of weeks and his wife-to-be's favorite restaurant is Beard's Bistro. Yesterday, he was talking about how a bunch of their friends were giving them a couple's shower there last night. He said he and his fiancée had just come back from the restaurant to make sure that everything was ready. He said the chef had assured them everything was under control, but I'll doublecheck it with him to make sure. Give me the best number where I can reach you."

Mike gave the chief his cell phone number and ended the call by saying, "Thanks, Chief. Anything you can find out would be a big help to me."

"Not a problem. If he's around, this shouldn't take too long."

Mike turned his attention back to driving. He often thought Oregon was one of the most beautiful places he'd ever been, and this particular scenic route only solidified that belief. He was enjoying the dense forests and peaceful atmosphere when his Bluetooth rang, indicating an incoming call.

He pressed a button on the dash. "This is Mike Reynolds."

"Mike, this is Chief Morgan. I told you this probably wouldn't take long, and it didn't. I was able to talk to my officer about the couples' shower at Beard's Bistro last night, and he said Chef Moore was front and center all night long. He confirmed that he and his fiancée had met with the chef at noon yesterday.

"My guy told me that the chef had stuck his head in the private room where the group was having dinner several times to make sure everything was going smoothly, and when it was over he personally went around to each table and thanked everyone for coming to his restaurant. My officer said the chef was a real showman and it was a class act."

"Sounds like it and that takes him out of the running as a possible murder suspect. Thanks, Chief. You saved me a trip. Don't know if

I'll be able to return the favor, but if you ever have a bad guy in Oregon you need some help with, you know the number."

"Mike, I've been around the block enough times to know that I probably will be calling on you at some point in time. Good luck finding the murderer, and while I'm glad I was able to help you eliminate one of the suspects, it still means there's a murderer out there somewhere, and I never like to hear that. Take care and be safe."

Mike ended the call, hoping that Kelly had found out something that might help. It had been more than twenty-four hours since Chef Jessup was murdered. That left about twenty-one more hours before the statistics kicked in, and their chances of solving the crime diminished substantially.

CHAPTER TWENTY

After Kelly's massage with Ramona, she wanted to see what she could find out about Alex Taylor and his wife. She left the spa and went back to the Gearhart Hotel, intending to do a search for them on her computer. When she walked in the front door, Dakota waved to her and called out, "Mrs. Reynolds, I have a message for you."

Kelly walked over to the reception desk and waited while Dakota gave recommendations to the couple in front of her as to where they could get the best fresh seafood in Seaside, the town just to the south of Gearhart. Kelly wondered how many times Dakota had recommended certain restaurants and wondered if she was compensated by them for doing so. She wasn't very proud of herself for thinking that but given the scarcity of high paying jobs in the vicinity, she thought it was a definite possibility.

Dakota told the couple to enjoy themselves and if they would like more recommendations during their stay, to feel free to ask her, then she turned to Kelly. "Mrs. Reynolds, Matt asked me to tell you he would like to see you in his office when you returned to the hotel. It's the second door on the left down that hallway."

"Thanks, Dakota. I'll go there before I go up to my room."

She knocked on the door and Matt said, "Come in." When he saw it was Kelly, he stood up and said, "I'll just keep you a minute. Why don't you sit over there? I think that view of the golf course is one of the best from anywhere in the hotel."

Kelly sat down and looked out the window. She glanced back towards Matt and agreed. "It's beautiful. If I were you I'd be very tempted to spend a lot of time sitting here rather than behind your desk, working."

"It's been known to happen, Mrs. Reynolds."

"Matt, please call me Kelly. Mrs. Reynolds sounds so formal and old."

"All right, I will. I don't know which to thank you for first, the huge help you were last night or loaning Rebel to my family."

"Is he doing all right?" Kelly asked anxiously.

"More than all right, although you definitely are the reason I'm going to have to replace him with a puppy. I went home for lunch to check and see how my family was doing. I can tell you unequivocally, Rebel is being spoiled beyond belief, but he appears to be thoroughly enjoying it. The children can't stop petting him. I had to tell them that dogs need time to sleep, and they promised me that they would give him some sleep time this afternoon."

Kelly relaxed. "I'm so glad. Even though he's a guard dog and can be quite intimidating, at heart he's a gentle soul and loves nothing more than to be spoiled. This trip is good for him since we have two younger dogs at home that are quite energetic. Being the only dog around and being spoiled is bound to make him feel special."

"I'm sure that's how he's feeling now, but I have to tell you a little story. When I went home for lunch I pressed the garage door opener and parked my car in the garage after waving to Bill, my security guard, who was parked down the street. As soon as I opened my car door I heard a growl. Then I heard Julie say, 'Rebel, it's okay. It's Matt. It's okay.' She opened the door to the garage and hugged me. As soon as Rebel saw that she'd given permission to someone to enter the house, he stopped growling and walked over to me, wagging his stubby little tail. We made friends, but I have to tell you if I was an intruder and I heard that deep growl, I wouldn't go anywhere near where that dog was."

"That's exactly why Mike wanted Rebel to be with your family during this difficult time. Believe me, you can be assured that nothing will happen to them while he's there."

"You have no idea how much that means to me. When I received the threat, I panicked. I wanted to be with my family, but I also knew I had to stay here, particularly given the murder."

"Have you heard anything from Chief Barnes about his son?" she asked.

"Not from him, but I stopped at the drugstore to get some aspirin. I think this whole thing has given me a headache, and Steve Cooper, the pharmacist there, told me that Kyle's son had been airlifted to Portland. That's all I know. Poor Kyle. He's a good guy."

"Oh dear," Kelly said. "I don't know if moving him to Portland is a good thing or a bad thing. Maybe it's nothing more than his doctor feeling that there would be more options in Portland than at a small hospital here."

"I'll keep that positive spin on it, Kelly, thanks. Anything I can do for you? I know Mike said he was going to Portland to check out some things."

"There is one thing," Kelly said. "What do you know about a guest of yours named Alex Taylor? I understand he's Bobby Lee's nephew. As you no doubt know, Bobby Lee is the owner of the Rotunda Hotel. I had lunch and a massage there."

"What did you think of it?" Matt asked.

"Quite honestly, I can't imagine the mindset of someone thinking that type of architecture would work in this setting, although the massage was great."

"You're not the only one with that opinion of the building. I hear that a lot, plus it's pretty pricey to stay there. As far as Alex Taylor goes, I'm not familiar with his name. I don't believe he's ever stayed here before. I didn't know Bobby had a nephew, so I can't be much help to you. Are you asking for a special reason?"

"I'm not sure. I know you probably have a policy of not giving out the room numbers of guests, but if you could check and give it to me, I'd appreciate it."

"You're right. That is completely against our policy, but in this case, since your husband's in charge of the murder investigation, I figure you're asking for a reason. Let me look at the computer for a moment." Matt pulled the room numbers of the guests up and said, "That's interesting. He's in room 205. That's directly across the hall from you." He looked at her and said, "Kelly, I don't know why you're asking, but if it involves the murder of Chef Jessup, please let Sheriff Reynolds handle it. Would you promise me that?"

"Certainly," she said brightly. "I was just curious. I need to go up to the room and do a little research. I like to help Mike whenever I can. Say hi to Rebel for me," she said as she stood up and walked over to the door. "Oh, one more question. Do you know Mrs. Lee?"

"I've met her at a couple of local events. They haven't been married very long. I don't like to gossip, but since you're asking me something about her, it might be related to the murder. Anyway, there's talk that she's getting ready to leave Bobby because the hotel isn't doing well. I've also heard it said that she and one of the masseurs at the hotel spa, I think his name is Andres Ramirez, have a more than casual interest in one another and that her massages with him may be that, but also a lot more. I can't verify either one of those things, Kelly, they're strictly rumors. Don't see where either one would fit in, but it might."

"Thanks, Matt."

CHAPTER TWENTY-ONE

Kelly walked up the stairway and paused in front of her room. She looked over at Room 205 and wondered how and when someone decided he was the reincarnation of James Beard. She shook her head, knowing there was far more to the human psyche than she'd ever learn.

When she was inside her room, she walked out to the balcony and looked at the golf course. Mike had told her only two rooms at the hotel had balconies, and although the view was beautiful, when compared to the one from Matt's office, it definitely came in second.

She was really looking forward to talking with Mike to see what he'd found out, but first she needed to do some research on Alex Taylor, Nikki Taylor, Amanda Lee, and Andres Ramirez.

She started with Alex Taylor.

From Google and Facebook, she confirmed what she'd already been told. Alex Taylor's Facebook page had an aka after his name – James Beard. The last few posts were rants about people cooking in the style of James Beard, and that he had not given them permission to do so. The more she read, the more she felt he really was unbalanced, and the post he'd made about people who said they were cooking in the style of James Beard should be eliminated, caused a shiver to run down her back.

If that's not a motive for murdering someone, I don't know what is. Actually, I think it's almost an admission of guilt before the crime has been made public.

She discovered that Alex had a Master's degree in food engineering, an offshoot of chemical engineering. He had worked for several years at a large food manufacturing company, but he'd recently been let go for unspecified reasons. Kelly tried to find out more about the reason for his dismissal, but she found nothing. She noted the date of his dismissal and compared it with the dates of the rants on his Facebook page. The rants had started about two months earlier. She thought that was more than a coincidence.

The next person she looked up was Nicole Taylor. She found out that Nicole worked as a chemist at the same food manufacturing company where Alex had worked. There was very little available about her. When Kelly pulled up her Facebook page, Nicole had put the bare minimum in, such as her education and that she was married. Her last post was over a year ago. Instead of a photograph of her she had chosen to use an avatar.

If Nicole's Facebook page had been sparse with personal information, Amanda Lee's page was the complete opposite. She was one of the legion of young women from small towns who had gone to Hollywood to become a movie star. She'd worked as a barmaid to support herself, but from what Kelly saw, the closest Amanda ever got to the big screen was as a paying customer at the neighborhood cinema.

The page was filled with photos of Amanda in different outfits, some quite scanty and suggestive, indicating she'd changed careers – from barmaid to pole dancer. The page showed that she had been married to Bobby Lee for almost a year, and even indicated that she'd been married twice before, but Bobby was the love of her life. There was a photo of the Rotunda Hotel, and in Amanda's words, "It is the most beautiful hotel in the Northwest and the star of Gearhart, Oregon, my new home."

From the number of posts she'd made in the past few days alone, it was apparent that Amanda devoted a great deal of her time and energy to keeping up her Facebook page. She had 5,000 friends and connections on Facebook, the maximum number of friends that Facebook allows an individual to have. Since she wasn't someone like a movie star or television personality, Kelly thought she probably had spent a lot of time inviting people to be her friends.

Lastly, she researched Andres Ramirez. There wasn't too much about him on Google other than the fact that he had emigrated to the United States from Columbia to join other family members. He was a U. S. citizen and worked as a massage therapist. She found several newspaper articles stating there were rumors that his uncle had been part of the Medellin drug cartel in the 1980's, but it had never been proven.

When she pulled up his Facebook page and saw Andres' picture, she understood why Ramona had referred to him as a Latin lover. His picture belonged more on the cover of GQ magazine than a Facebook page. It was obvious from his shirtless picture that he worked out regularly, which along with his dark complexion, jet black hair worn in a man bun, and smoldering deep brown eyes, made him look like a female magnet. Kelly thought there was a very good chance that Ramona was right. He looked like the type of man who would appeal to Amanda.

As long as I'm here, she thought, *might as well see what I can find out about Bobby Lee. His name wasn't in Chef Jessup's diary, but neither were Amanda, Nicole, nor Andres.*

When she Googled him, she found out that his mother, brother, sister, and him had emigrated to the United States from China when the children were teenagers. His father had been a prominent political figure, but a scandal had forced him out of office, and he was later imprisoned for embezzlement. His mother worried that her children would be tainted by their father's actions and came to the United States to be with some of her relatives.

Bobby's mother had been so grateful for the warm welcome her family had received in the United States that she and her children became U.S. citizens. The article she read said Bobby had become quite successful in real estate and had decided to build a high-end hotel and spa in Gearhart, Oregon. It went on to say that the design theme of the hotel was a tribute to his new home, the United States, a thank you for giving him the chance to become a millionaire. It also indicated that the hotel was not doing as well as Bobby had expected and that his fortune had decreased dramatically in the last few months.

According to the article, Bobby Lee had met the woman of his dreams, Amanda, through mutual friends. Several times he had stated in different articles that he had to be the happiest man in the world. He was married to the most beautiful woman in the world, and he owned the most beautiful hotel in the world.

Seems like a bit of a stretch on both accounts, Kelly thought. *That hotel has to be the gaudiest, most out-of-place hotel I've ever seen. And I hate to think it, but Amanda looks like she's been, as the old saying about a horse goes, rode hard and put away wet.*

Just then her cell phone rang and when she picked it up, she saw Mike's name flash up on the screen. "Hey, Sheriff, I was beginning to wonder what happened to you. Where are you?"

"I'm about thirty miles away, but I want to stop by the station and see if there's an update on Kyle's son. I should be back to the hotel within the hour. It's been an interesting day. How was yours?"

"Illuminating, but I'm not sure what to make out of what I've learned, if that makes any sense."

"Clear as mud, darling. Maybe by sharing what we've both learned today, we'll see a little daylight. Gotta go, Kelly. I've got another call. Bye, love you."

Even though she'd had a great massage, Kelly felt like she needed to do something physical. Maybe that would help her fit the pieces of the puzzle together. She decided to walk over to the coffee shop she'd seen on the way to the hotel when they arrived yesterday.

Kelly walked back out onto the balcony to see what the weather was like. Even though it was summer, and the day had been balmy, the fog had started to come in. She decided a light jacket would probably be a good thing to take with her.

Whenever she was on a trip, she always liked to go to coffee shops and see if she could pick up any tips on how to make Kelly's Koffee Shop better, although given the popularity of it, it seemed like she was doing everything right. She walked into the shop and was immediately greeted by a woman's voice, "Welcome. You can place your order here, and I'll bring it to you. It's late in the day so we're out of a lot of things, but I'm sure you'll find something you can't pass up."

Kelly walked over to the glass-enclosed display counter stuffed with mouth-watering goodies and thought, *if this is what it looks like when they're out of things, I can't imagine what it looks like first thing in the morning.* She ordered a mocha latte and a large peanut butter cookie. *Caffeine and sugar, this should keep me going for a while.* After she'd placed her order, she walked over to a window table. She noticed several of the outdoor tables were occupied with people and their dogs.

She spent several minutes looking out the window at them and an idea began to take shape. *I've got a good relationship with the dock owner where Kelly's is located. I'll bet he'd be okay with me putting a few tables in front of the coffee shop. I could put water bowls out for customers' dogs and even have gourmet dog cookies for sale. It would probably bring in some new people who want to eat at a place where they can take their dog. I'll make that a priority when I get back to Cedar Bay.*

She finished her latte and walked back to the hotel, the puzzle concerning the murder of Samantha Jessup still unsolved.

CHAPTER TWENTY-TWO

Kelly returned to the hotel from the coffee shop and took the stairs that led to the second floor where her room was located. When she got to the top of the stairs, she heard loud voices coming from the room across the hall from hers. Alex Taylor's room. She held her breath and paused to listen.

"Alex, I mean it. This craziness has got to stop. It's already cost you your job, and I'm about ready to see if I can have you committed. Thinking you're the reincarnation of James Beard is not normal, and I'm sure I can find a doctor who would agree with me."

Kelly recognized the voice as being that of Nikki, the woman who had been with Amanda Lee at lunch.

"Yeah, you think you're so high and mighty, just because you got the promotion and raise. You know it never would have happened if I hadn't gotten you that job. Now that I'm James Beard, and no longer Alex Taylor, you don't want anything to do with me. You've become a real nag, Nikki," Alex said angrily.

"I can't go on like this, Alex. I'm giving you one week to get rid of this James Beard thing and find a job, or I'm out of here."

"Nikki, I know how much you like money. Isn't that the real reason you're angry that I'm not with that stupid food manufacturing company anymore? Admit it."

"Alex, yes, money is important to me. It's what provides a roof over your head and food in your stomach. I kind of consider those things to be important. One more week and that's it."

"When I get the money from Uncle Bobby, you won't be saying that. You won't need to worry about money. I did a favor for Uncle Bobby."

"You're talking like the crazy man you've become. What kind favor? I had lunch with Amanda today, and she never said anything about you doing a favor for him. Why are you smiling like that?" Nikki asked.

"Because I know something neither one of you knows. Just Uncle Bobby's and my secret. As a matter of fact, I think this secret will let me take over the restaurant at Uncle Bobby's hotel. I think I'll change the name to The Real James Beard Restaurant. Yes, once I have the restaurant, people will flock to Uncle Bobby's hotel. It will be the hotel and restaurant that everyone will want to go to and eat at. Anyway, I'm late. I have an appointment with Uncle Bobby. You'll see, Nikki. This will all work out for the best."

Kelly quickly opened the door to her room, stepped inside, and closed the door. She looked through the peephole in the door and saw a man she presumed was Alex Taylor leave the room across the hall. She heard his steps as he went down the stairs and then there was quiet. Kelly didn't know what to do, but she felt this might be the perfect time to talk to Nikki.

She left her room and tentatively knocked on the door across the hall. "Who is it?" a tearful voice called out.

"It's Kelly Reynolds. I'm your neighbor across the hall. Could I talk to you for a minute?"

It was quiet inside the room and then Kelly heard the sounds of footsteps, and a moment later, the door opened. It was Nikki, the woman she'd seen earlier in the day with Amanda. Where her makeup had been perfectly in place then, now her face was almost unrecognizable because of the damage her tears had done to it.

"What do you want?" she asked Kelly in an irritated tone of voice.

"Nikki, may I come in? I know you're having some problems, and I thought you might like to talk to someone. I couldn't help but overhear the argument between you and your husband a few moments ago."

Nikki scowled. "Why would you care what's going on between my husband and me? I don't even know you."

The door was far enough open that Kelly could enter, and she walked in, Nikki making no effort to stop her. "Nikki, there's a lot I can't tell you, and for that I'm sorry. I can only imagine what you're going through. I will tell you that I agree with you that Alex has become mentally unstable."

"What makes you say that?" Nikki's words were shaky. "You don't know anything about us."

"I know that you're a very honorable woman who has, through no fault of your own, become involved in a situation that is totally out of your control. I know that your husband thinks he's the reincarnation of James Beard, and that he's lost his job."

"How do you know all of that?" Nikki asked, wide-eyed.

Kelly was debating how much to tell her, because she wasn't at liberty to reveal anything about Chef Jessup's murder. "I was at the Rotunda Hotel having lunch today and happened to be seated near you and Mrs. Lee. I couldn't help but overhear your conversation, and what I heard a few minutes ago only confirms that your husband is deeply disturbed and perhaps mentally deranged. Why don't you sit down and tell me about it? Maybe I can help."

Nikki sat down heavily in a chair by the window and Kelly sat across from her.

"I really don't want to unload on a stranger," Nikki sighed, "but I guess it doesn't matter now. All anybody has to do is be around Alex for a few minutes to see that he's gone off the deep end."

"When did it start?"

"We live in Portland and there was an article in The Oregonian about a restaurant that had been written up as the best in Portland. It's called The Pampered Hamburger. The article said the food was prepared by a chef who gave homage to James Beard by preparing every dish in his style. Alex wanted to go there for dinner. That was when it all started."

"Had Alex ever talked about James Beard before?" Kelly asked.

"No more than anyone else in this area. We often visited his Uncle Bobby when he was building the Rotunda Hotel and then after he opened it. While we were here we'd go to Seaside and Cannon Beach. James Beard spent a lot of summers here, so his name is well known in this area."

"When did you realize something was wrong?"

Nikki paused while she thought for a few seconds. "After we ate dinner at The Pampered Hamburger, he became a different man. I don't know what happened, actually I doubt that anyone could pinpoint the exact moment someone snaps, but the morning after we ate there he told me that he'd had a dream that had been a revelation to him. He said that a spirit had come to him and told him in the dream that he was James Beard." She sat back and looked at Kelly.

"What did you say?"

Nikki shrugged. "What does anyone say when someone makes a statement like that? I told him that was crazy talk. I told him I knew James Beard had been dead for over thirty years, and if he was going to come back, he'd probably come back in the form of a chef who owned a restaurant. That's when he told me that was exactly what he planned to do when he got enough money.

"It went downhill from there. All he talked about at work was James Beard, and after being called into his manager's office several times and admonished for it, he was given his pink slip and two week's severance pay. The weird thing about it was that he was really happy he'd been fired. The night after it happened, he told me that now he could totally devote himself to his restaurant."

"What kind of plans was he making towards that end?"

"He spent hours on the internet looking at restaurants for sale and buildings for rent that might be suitable for a restaurant. He narrowed his search to Cannon Beach, Seaside, and Gearhart. He told me a lot of James Beard's fans visited this area, and they would all come to his restaurant."

"Did he decide on a place or rent one?"

"No. Something happened about a week ago, and I don't know what it was. He began to say that Uncle Bobby was making everything possible, but he wouldn't give me any specifics. The only other thing he said was that it was time for the Beard wannabes to leave this earth. I thought that sounded kind of ominous, but when I asked him what he meant, he refused to tell me." She started to cry softly.

Kelly went into the bathroom and got a tissue for her as well as a glass of water. "Have you told anyone about this?" she asked, when Nikki was settled.

"No. I talked to Amanda at lunch, as you evidently overheard, but other than that no one. I was afraid if my boss ever found out he'd think I was as loony as Alex has become, and he'd fire me, too. With Alex not working, we need my salary more than ever."

Kelly considered what Nikki had just told her. "How do you think Uncle Bobby fits into all of this?"

"I've tried and tried to figure it out, but I can't. Alex is his sister's child, that's why they don't share the last name. His sister died when Alex was quite young. His father remarried, and from what Alex told me his new wife hated Alex. After about a year, Alex went to live with his Uncle Bobby. He paid for Alex to go to college, and Alex has always felt he owed his uncle. Beyond that, I don't know."

"Has Alex ever had previous mental problems?"

Nikki was quiet for several moments, and then she spoke up. "I understand he had some issues when his father remarried. Once he mentioned that he would never go back to a mental institution, no matter what happened in his life. When I asked him what he meant, he blew it off, as if it was nothing. He's also been really paranoid lately. He told me once that he had an illegal wiretap put on his phone, so he'd have evidence if anyone ever tried to pin something on him."

"That does sound a bit paranoid. What about a history of violence?"

Nikki shook her head so fast several strands of her long dark hair obscured her face. She brushed them away with her hand. "Certainly not with me. That's one thing I would never put up with. Other than saying someone should get rid of the wannabe James Beard chefs, I can't think of anything."

They were both quiet for a few moments. Kelly looked at her watch and realized Mike would be returning to the hotel momentarily, if he wasn't already in their room. "Nikki, I'm just across the hall. If you need anything, please feel free to ask me." She stood up and then reached down to put her hand on Nikki's shoulder. "Do you think you should leave and go somewhere until Alex gets help?"

"You're thinking he could be dangerous, aren't you?" Nikki asked. "The answer is no, unfortunately. I have no family to speak of, and with the hours I work, I have no social life. Don't worry. I'll be fine. Hopefully, this is just a phase."

"For your sake, I hope so," Kelly said, "but please remember my offer. You know where to find me."

"I will, and thanks for listening to me. Most people wouldn't have taken the extra step needed to help someone in my predicament. I appreciate it."

CHAPTER TWENTY-THREE

Kelly walked back across the hall and unlocked the door to their room. As soon as she entered the room she was swept up in a big bear hug. "What's that all about, Mike?" she asked as she hugged him back.

"I just missed you today. This was supposed to be your birthday weekend, and instead, I went to Portland, and you did whatever else. Believe me, this is not what I had planned." He reluctantly released her. "We were going to explore this whole coastal area, go see Haystack Rock in Cannon Beach and then visit Ecola Park. Instead we've done nothing but try to solve a murder. You'd think just once the powers of the universe would let us have a real vacation."

Kelly set her purse on the bed. "Guess we just racked up some bad karma. I could use a break from this murder investigation, and I'm sure you could as well. When I came back to the room, I saw that someone had put a bottle of Pinot Noir wine on the dresser for us. Maybe Matt instructed the cleaning crew to do it. What say we share a glass out on the balcony and watch the last golfers of the day?"

"Consider it done. I'll join you out there in a minute. I want to wash up and then I'll be right back."

A few minutes later he walked out onto the balcony and handed her a glass of wine. "To my favorite birthday girl. May you have many, many more and may I be around to toast you for all of them," he said touching his glass with hers.

"Well, if you're going to be around to toast me for all of them, sounds like you want to outlive me," she said laughing.

"No, Kelly," Mike said in a serious tone of voice. "You're the best thing that's ever happened to me, and I love you more than I ever thought possible. Believe me, I do not want to outlive you. I can't imagine you not being around. I don't even want to think about it. Let's change the subject. Tell me about your day."

She started with the effect Rebel had on the Parker family and what Matt had told her about Rebel growling at him when he tried to get in his own house.

"Sounds like Rebel, but I feel a lot better with him there, and I'm sure Matt does too. Having your family threatened and not being with them has to be a terrifying thought," Mike said.

"Yes, I'm sure it is, but we might want to figure out what we're going to do with a dog who has become completely spoiled. I have a sense those children are doing nothing but that."

"Rebel's an old dog, and with Lady and Skyy, I'm sure he's had his challenges. Being special for a few days won't hurt him at all. Poor old guy could probably use a little extra TLC," Mike said. "Find out anything of interest when you were at the Rotunda Hotel today?"

"A lot, but first let me tell you who I had breakfast with."

"Okay, I'll bite. Who did you have breakfast with?"

"None other than one of the people on our list, Jessica Cartland, but I have to tell you, I think we can take her off the list. I'm certain she had nothing to do with the murder."

"And why is that?"

She told him about her conversation with Jessica and concluded by saying, "She'll be writing a couple of articles for The Oregonian on the James Beard dinner and James Beard. In it she's going to really talk up Chef Jessup. Quite frankly, I felt a little guilty letting her go on about it. I don't know what she'll think when she finds out that Chef Jessup had been murdered prior to the dinner, and that she didn't have anything to do with its preparation."

"Don't forget she's a newswoman. It's probably not the first time she's had to rewrite something based on changing events. However, I do agree with you. Think we can cross her off, and I have a couple of others to strike off as well."

"Okay, your turn. When you're finished, I'll tell you about my afternoon, beginning with lunch."

"Fair enough." Mike rubbed his stomach. "I went to The Pioneer Grill and had one of the best sandwiches of my life. I also found out that Chef Stevenson, Chef Jessup's ex-husband, was at the restaurant yesterday at the time of the murder. The only odd thing was my waiter, who was quite close to the chef, telling me that Chef Stevenson had mentioned receiving threats, something about being a wannabe James Beard. My waiter said that the chef had just shrugged them off, saying there were a lot of wackos out there, or words to that effect."

Kelly sipped her wine, the rich fruity taste soothing her, although not as much as the massage had done. "I have to tell you, Mike, that I never knew James Beard had such a following. I mean restaurants named after one of his favorite foods, dinners in his honor, people who say they're James Beard's reincarnation. It's kind of unbelievable."

"You heard that someone thinks they're the reincarnation of James Beard?" A look of surprise crossed Mike's face.

"I did, and I'll fill you in on that when you're finished. What was next?"

"After lunch and crossing off Chef Stevenson from my list of possible suspects, I debated whether I should drive or fly to San Francisco. I knew I needed to determine the whereabouts of Daniel Moore yesterday. I was trying to figure out what I should do when I remembered that Baker to Vegas Relay Race from last year. You know, the one where we were beaten by that relay team from SFPD? Like by only five minutes? Anyway, I had Chief Morgan's number, and I thought maybe he could help me. Turned out that call saved me a trip."

"That was good thinking. Was he any help?"

"Huge. Here's what he found out." Mike told her about the couples' shower and then said, "So, that's one more name we can eliminate. Of course, either one of them could have hired someone else to commit murder, but I'm inclined to let them go. Now it's your turn."

She spent the next half hour telling him everything that had taken place, from her lunch at the Rotunda Hotel to her recent conversation with Nikki. When she was finished, she said, "So, what do you think?"

Mike was quiet for almost a minute as he thought about what Kelly had just told him. Finally, he said, "I'm all over the board here. Bobby might have wanted Chef Jessup dead so there would be some bad publicity, but I don't see him getting his hands dirty. Certainly, Alex is rising to the top of the suspect list. He's got a motive, and it sounds like he's suffering from some type of a mental breakdown."

"Yes, but what do you think about his references to Uncle Bobby and that he'd done a favor for him?" Kelly asked.

"This is pretty twisted on all accounts, but maybe Bobby asked Alex to murder Samantha. Alex would probably be all for it, given her ties to James Beard, and Bobby hoped that the bad publicity would destroy his main hotel competition and make his hotel a success. As I said, it's pretty twisted, but it's all I can come up with at the moment."

"Where do you think Amanda or Andres fits into this, if at all? According to Ramona, Amanda is having an affair with him, but I don't see any reason for them to murder the chef."

"Nor do I," Mike said. "Seems to me it was to Amanda's benefit to have Bobby make a go of the hotel. The one thing we don't know is how serious the affair is. You did find out that Andres has family ties to people who have been involved in a lot of violence. I could see Andres having Bobby murdered, but why Chef Jessup? No, I don't see a nexus there."

"One other thing, Mike. You mentioned that your waiter at lunch told you that Chef Stevenson had received some threats. I wonder if Chef Moore did? What I'm thinking is that in Chef Jessup's diary she mentioned something about Alex making a threat. Maybe he made threats to several well-known chefs who were known for cooking in the style of James Beard. And if that's so, don't you think they should be warned?"

"That's a very good point, Kelly, but here's the problem." Mike twisted his glass around by the stem. "Chief Barnes hasn't made the murder of Samantha Jessup public, and I don't have the authority to do it. I would really be stepping on his toes if I did something like that. It's just not done. This is his jurisdiction, and until he decides to make it public, my hands are tied. I wonder how his son is doing. I've thought about calling him, but I'm sure his priority right now is his son and his family."

"Mike, I'm sorry. I forgot to tell you that Matt told me he heard from the town pharmacist that Chief Barnes' son had been airlifted to Portland. No one knew whether that's a good thing or a bad thing. Could have been good because he can probably get better care, but on the other hand, it might not be good if they thought it was serious enough they had to get him to Portland. Other than that, I've heard nothing."

"Birthday girl, I have a proposition for you. If you let me order room service and then let me go to bed so I can get some much-needed sleep, I promise when this is over I'll buy you a fabulous meal somewhere, and we'll really celebrate your birthday. I'm whipped, and the mere thought of changing clothes and going downstairs to the restaurant does not appeal to me. Would you indulge me this favor, and then I'll be yours for life?"

Kelly nudged his knee. "Mike, I feel the same way. I'm tired, my brain is going a million miles an hour, and I don't know what to make of any of this. Let's phone in our order and get a good night's shut-eye. I don't think either one of us did very well in the sleep department last night."

CHAPTER TWENTY-FOUR

The following morning Kelly woke up to the smell of coffee and a note on the pillow where Mike slept. "Good morning, my love. Here's a cup of coffee for you. There's more in the hall. I've gone to the station to write a report before I forget anything. Figure that's the least I can do for Chief Barnes. I should be back by ten or so. We can have breakfast then."

Kelly reluctantly got out of bed. She would have preferred to stay there a little longer, but the siren call of more coffee won out. She decided a shower would help her to wake up and getting dressed was probably a good option before she went out into the hallway for her coffee.

A few minutes later, she opened her door and walked over to the table where the coffee urn was sitting on a small table. She was filling her coffee cup when she heard a scream come from Nikki's room. She put the cup down and walked over to the door.

"You what?" She heard Nikki yell. "You killed her? You are crazy, really crazy, Alex! Why did you do that? Why are you telling me this? I don't want to know. And what is that, a gun?"

"I did it for Uncle Bobby and the money. He's going to pay me well for killing Chef Jessup. In fact, he's already paid me $5,000. Keep your voice down, Nikki. You know things haven't been very good between us for a while. I've been thinking if you weren't around to constantly make fun of me, my life would be a lot easier. You won't need to worry about me working any more. I'll have all the money I need to live on, thanks to Uncle Bobby."

"Are you going to kill me?" Nikki asked in a shrill voice.

"Uncle Bobby gave me the idea. Well, he doesn't actually know I'm going to kill you, but he'll probably guess. I'm going to have to kill Uncle Bobby's chef, too. Once he's gone, as James Beard I'll take my rightful place in the restaurant. Oh, yeah, I need to kill a couple of other chefs as well. They're worthless imposters of me and need to be eliminated so there won't be any confusion about who the real James Beard is. It's really not that big a deal. I'm sure they'll want to come back as someone else, just like I did. If they could, they'd probably thank me."

Kelly couldn't believe what she was hearing. There was absolutely no doubt in her mind that Alex Taylor was crazy, certifiably insane, and definitely dangerous. She had to do something to help Nikki. There was a housekeeping closet next to Nikki's room. Maybe there was something in it that she could use. She opened the door to the closet and took out the first thing that came to hand, which was a broom. She had no idea what she was going to do with it, and she knew she didn't have any time to waste.

"Alex, think about this." Nikki's high-pitched voice carried clearly to where Kelly was standing in the hallway. "People will hear the gun go off, and you won't be able to get away. You'll be arrested for murder. Leave now, and I promise you that I will never tell anyone about this conversation. You can have everything in the house, as well as our checking and savings accounts. Clean them out. Just let me live," she begged tearfully. "I don't want to die."

In one quick motion Kelly threw open the door, raised the broom, and without even thinking, used the pole to smash the gun out of Alex's hand. It slithered across the floor and she yelled, "Nikki, get the gun." Nikki reached down and picked it up, clearly uncomfortable with it. "Give it to me," Kelly said in a commanding tone of voice. She dropped the broom, took the gun and pointed it at Alex, her hand steady.

"I don't want to use this, but I'm very good with a gun. Just stand against the wall with your hands up. One move and I'll shoot." She cocked her head towards Nikki. "Nikki, go into my room and get the phone that's on the dresser. Bring it back here."

A moment later Nikki returned with Kelly's phone. "Nikki, press the favorites, then press the name Mike and hand the phone to me."

A moment later she heard Mike's voice, "Kelly, I trust you got my note. The chief returned this morning, and he and I are headed to the hotel. I filled him in on what's happened on my end, but he'd like to talk to you."

"Mike, hurry. I'm holding a gun on Alex. He admitted he killed Chef Jessup. Hurry."

"On my way. Where are you?"

"I'm in Alex and Nikki's room across the hall from ours."

Less than a minute later Kelly heard footsteps charging up the stairs and Matt rushed into the room. "Are you all right, Kelly? Mike just called and told me to get up to Nikki's room as fast as possible. He and the chief will be here momentarily." He stepped beside her. "Hand me the gun. I'm a hunter and an expert shot."

Kelly heard Mike's voice a few minutes later as he and Chief Barnes ran up the stairs. "We're here, Kelly. Everything's going to be okay," he yelled. He ran into the room and over to her, hugging her as if he never wanted to let her go. "Are you all right?" he asked, patting her anxiously.

She brushed his hands away. "Yes, I'm fine. Fortunately, there was a housekeeping closet next to their room, and I was able to knock the gun out of Alex's hand with a heavy broom. Oh, Mike, he was going to kill Nikki. I had to do something," she said tearfully, as the gravity of the situation sunk in and she began to tremble.

Chief Barnes handcuffed Alex and made him sit on the floor while the chief called his sergeant and ordered him and two deputies to come to the hotel. When they arrived, he told them to take Alex to the station, read him his Miranda rights, and book him for murder and attempted murder.

For the next hour Kelly and Nikki answered the chief's questions, gave statements, and with a deep sense of thanksgiving thought about what they'd escaped. When they were done the chief said, "Kelly, Mike, I can never thank you enough for solving this murder. I'm sorry I had to ask you to take charge, but I didn't have a choice."

"Chief, I haven't heard. How is your son?" Kelly asked.

"Much, much better. He came out of the coma, and it looks like he'll have a full recovery. He's going to stay at the hospital in Portland for at least a week. They want to run more tests and make sure everything's all right before they release him."

"I'm so glad. I really have been sending healing thoughts to him and your family."

"Thanks. Maybe that's what helped." He turned towards Mike. "Hate to ask this, but as you know, we're a very small force. I need to arrest Bobby Lee for being the mastermind behind Chef Jessup's murder. Soliciting for a murder is a felony, and I intend to charge him with first degree murder. Anyway, I could use a backup. I don't think Bobby Lee is the kind of guy who keeps a gun in his office, but I don't want to be surprised. Would you mind going with me?"

"Not at all. Might as well do it now before he hears about Alex's arrest. Kelly, I'll be back later. I'd kind of like to get back to Cedar Bay this afternoon. Matt, would it be okay if we stop by and pick up Rebel when I finish up with the Bobby Lee arrest?"

"Absolutely. I'll call my wife and tell her. When do you think you'll be there?"

Mike looked at his watch. "After we arrest Bobby Lee and take him to the station, I'll have someone drive me back here to the hotel. Kelly can pack for me, so I'd say around two."

"I'll be there. I have a little something I need to pick up and take home anyway. By the way, it goes without saying that your room and everything else here at the Gearhart Hotel has been comped. We've backed out any charges to your credit card such as the dinner and the hotel deposit." Matt added, "I can't thank you enough for everything you've done."

"Glad I could help." Mike smiled and turned to the chief. "Okay, Chief Barnes. Let's get this over with."

At 2:00 that afternoon Mike and Kelly pulled up in front of the Parkers' house. From the looks of it, Matt had arrived moments before. He waved to them and called them over. "Let me get the group out here. I have something I think they're going to be very happy about."

Matt hurried up to the front door and a few minutes later Julie, Kayla, and Aiden walked out behind him. He told them to stand on the porch while he got something out of his car for them. Rebel had come out with them and eagerly walked over to where Mike and Kelly were standing.

Matt opened the passenger door of the car and picked something up from a box in the front seat. When he turned around, he was carrying a fawn colored boxer puppy, a miniature replica of Rebel.

"Dad," screamed Kayla, her freckled face lighting up. "Is that little baby puppy ours?"

"Sure is. I'm going to put her down on the ground for a few minutes, because she's been in the car for a little while." They all watched while the little puppy raced around, sniffing her new surroundings, ran up to where Kayla and Aiden were standing, and promptly laid down and fell asleep. Aiden reached down and picked her up.

Aiden looked up at his father. "Dad, can I take her in the house, so she can get used to things?" he asked.

"Yes, I have her food, a water dish, and a dog bed in the car. I'll bring them in shortly, but first I need to say goodbye to Kelly and Mike." Matt turned to them and said, "I can't ever thank you enough for helping me protect my family. I'll never forget either one of you, and certainly not Rebel," he said as he reached down and patted the big dog on his head and scratched his ears.

"I feel the same way," Julie said, gripping Matt's hand. "That dog has wrapped himself around all of our hearts." She turned to Matt. "You never said anything about getting a puppy. How did that happen?"

"I was in the pharmacy yesterday and mentioned something about getting a dog to Mac. He said that was quite a coincidence because his boxer had given birth to a litter, and they were about ready to start looking for homes for them. I went out to his house yesterday afternoon and bought the pup. I told him I wasn't sure when I could pick her up and asked if Mac could take care of her for a couple more days or so. After the events of this morning, I decided to bring the pup home while Kelly and Mike were here picking up Rebel. I thought it might be too hard on the kids to have him leave."

"Matt, I had no idea you were thinking of doing something like that," Julie said.

"Quite frankly, neither did I," Matt said ruefully. "Guess the universe decided it was time."

"Rebel, time to go home," Mike said. He turned back to Matt and shook his hand. "Glad everything worked out. Given that Bobby Lee was behind all of this, don't think you'll get a shred of bad publicity from it."

"Nor do I. Again, thanks for everything."

Kelly, Rebel, and Mike got in the car and headed towards their home in Cedar Bay.

When they were on the road, Mike glanced sideways at Kelly. "Well, birthday girl. This weekend wasn't quite what I had planned, but it was a birthday you probably will remember for a long time. And don't forget, I owe you a birthday dinner."

"Trust me, Sheriff, I won't."

EPILOGUE

"Kelly," Mike said as he walked in the house from the garage, followed by Skyy, Lady, and Rebel, all hoping that his next stop would be the dog cookie jar. "I heard from Chief Barnes today. I've got a lot to tell you." He kissed the back of her neck as she stood over the stove, stirring something that smelled delicious. Then he went to the cookie jar with the paw print on it and took three dog cookies out of it.

Kelly turned around and rubbed her hands on her pink apron embroidered with a red "Hot Stuff" motif. "I want to hear all about it. I've thought about the people we met in Gearhart many, many times. Some were good, some were bad, but all of them were interesting, and all are certainly burned into my memory."

"Let me get out of my uniform. I'll be back in a minute." He returned wearing jeans and a T-shirt. "This feels ever so much better. The weather's turning cold, and a glass of red wine has been calling to me all day. Can I interest you in the same?"

"Yes, thanks. Now tell me everything," she said as she sat across from him at the kitchen table.

"First of all, Bobby and Alex were both charged with first degree murder. Their trials are coming up shortly. The chief is hoping for a guilty verdict in both of their cases, although Alex will probably get off because he's almost certainly going to be found insane.

"Secondly, some guy named Gino Ferrari, he's out of Las Vegas, took over the Rotunda Hotel and, according to the chief, has poured a ton of money into advertising. It's actually starting to make a profit, or so the chief thinks, based on the number of people with out-of-states plates he's seen in the hotel's parking lot."

"Hear anything about Nikki?" Kelly asked.

"Yes. I guess she's really well-known in her field and was hired by a food company in Boston as a vice-president. Kyle said she's divorced Alex and moved there."

"I wish her well. Probably a good idea for her to leave Portland. I would think there would be too many memories there for her," Kelly said. "I kind of wondered if Paul would feel that way, but I've talked to him several times and he seems to really enjoy being the owner and head chef of The Pampered Hamburger. I liked him."

"I did too. Let's see, am I leaving anyone out?"

"What about Amanda and Andres? Did they run off into the sunset together?"

"I knew there was something else," Mike said, snapping his fingers in the air. "You're going to love this. Amanda divorced Bobby, and she's living with Gino. As for Andres. He disappeared right after Bobby was arrested, and no one has seen him around. Maybe he went back to Columbia."

"What about that food critic, Jessica Cartland? Hear anything about her?"

"Yes, that was another one the chief mentioned. She'd called him and asked why the murder hadn't been promptly reported. She said she'd written an article about how wonderful the James Beard dinner was, and she felt like a fool after she found out that Chef Jessup hadn't prepared it."

"I think I told you I felt bad about that, but it wasn't my place to tell her anything," Kelly reminded him.

"This ought to make you feel better. According to the chief, when Jessica found out she went to The Pampered Hamburger to talk to Paul. He'd read her favorable article, and they talked for a long time. One thing led to another and now they're seeing each other."

"You're kidding! I thought he hated her."

"Well, people do change, and I guess this is a case in point. Oh, and one more thing. Kyle and Matt see each other a lot and Daisy, the little boxer Matt got for his family, has become quite the hit of Gearhart. The family takes her everywhere. Matt often has her in his office when the kids are in school and Julie's teaching. Think that's everything."

"No." Kelly wagged her finger. "You left one thing out. My birthday dinner. I still haven't collected on that."

"I'm working on it, Kelly, I'm working on it."

Kelly looked at him and rolled her eyes. "Maybe we can make a deal. How about you don't have to take me out to dinner if you promise to tell me I don't look a year older."

Mike grinned. "Deal. Shake."

RECIPES
(FROM THE JAMES BEARD FOUNDATION)

BROWNIE CRINKLES

Ingredients:
4 oz. unsweetened chocolate, chopped
4 eggs, jumbo, at room temperature
1 tsp. pure vanilla extract
1 ¾ cups all-purpose flour
¼ cup Dutch processed cocoa powder
1 ½ tsp. baking powder
1 tsp. kosher salt
1 tsp. sea salt flakes (I like Maldon)
½ cup canola or sunflower oil
1 ¾ cups cane sugar

Coating Ingredient:
1 cup confectioners' sugar, sifted

Directions:
In a heatproof bowl set over (but not touching) barely simmering water in a pan, melt the chocolate, stirring occasionally with a rubber spatula. Keep the chocolate warm.

Crack the eggs into a bowl and add the vanilla. In a separate bowl, whisk the flour, cocoa, baking powder, and salts together.

In the bowl of a stand mixer fitted with the paddle attachment, mix the oil and sugar on low speed for 1 minute. Add the melted chocolate and mix to combine, approximately 30 seconds. Scrape the sides and bottom of the bowl with a rubber spatula. On medium speed, add the eggs and vanilla, one egg at a time, mixing briefly to incorporate before adding the next one, approximately 5 seconds for each egg. Scrape the sides and bottom of the bowl with a rubber spatula to bring the batter together. Mix on medium speed for 20 to 30 second to make nearly homogenous.

Add the dry ingredients all at once and mix until the dough comes together but still looks shaggy, approximately 30 seconds. Do not overmix. Remove the bowl from the stand mixer. With a plastic dough scraper, bring the dough completely together by hand and put in a small bowl. Cover the bowl with plastic wrap and refrigerate until the dough is firm, at least 30 minutes or overnight.

Heat the oven to 350 degrees and line a couple of cookie sheets with parchment paper.

Make the coating: Put the confectioners' sugar in a bowl, ensuring there is plenty of room in the bowl to roll the dough in the sugar. Using a melon or small ice cream scoop, roll the dough into small balls.

Coat the balls completely and generously with the confectioners' sugar. (You won't be using all of the sugar.) The dough should resemble snowballs.

Evenly space the balls on the prepared cookie sheets. Add a couple of generous pinches more of confectioners' sugar to the tops. Bake for 8 minutes. Rotate the pan and bake for another 3 to 4 minutes. The cookies will form crinkles and will be set in the middle. Let the cookies cool on the pan for 1 to 2 minutes, then transfer them to a wire rack to cool. The cookies can be stored in an airtight container at room temperature for up to 3 days. The dough can be refrigerated for up to 1 week.

CHICKEN WITH FORTY CLOVES OF GARLIC

Ingredients:
8 – 10 chicken legs
2/3 cup olive oil
2 tsps. salt
¼ tsp. pepper
Dash of nutmeg
40 cloves garlic, approximately 3 bulbs, peeled
4-6 stalks celery, thinly sliced
6 parsley sprigs
1 tbsp. dried tarragon
¼ cup dry vermouth
Pumpernickel bread

Directions:
Preheat oven to 375 degrees. Rinse the chicken legs in cold water and pat dry with paper towels. Dip the chicken in olive oil to coat each piece and sprinkle with salt, pepper, and nutmeg.

Put the chicken in a lidded 3-quart casserole along with the residue of oil. Add the garlic, sliced celery, parsley, tarragon, and vermouth. Seal the top of the casserole with a sheet of foil and cover tightly. Bake for 1 ½ hours. Do not remove the lid while baking. Serve with hot toast or thin slices of Pumpernickel bread and spread the softened garlic on the bread.

TOMATO SOUP WITH RICOTTA AND CRISPY BACON

Ingredients:
1 large garlic clove
¼ tsp. fine sea salt
Olive oil – about a splash
2 ¼ pounds ripe tomatoes
½ cup hot vegetable broth, plus more to taste (About ½ cup.)
1 tbsp. balsamic vinegar
1 tbsp. tomato paste

1 bay leaf
Pinch of sugar
Ground pepper to taste
1 small handful of fresh basil leaves, very thinly sliced
3-4 slices bacon (use 4 slices for 4 appetizer portions)
4 to 8 heaping teaspoons fresh ricotta
8 to 12 small fresh basil leaves
A few black peppercorns, crushed with a mortar and pestle (I usually put them in a plastic bag and use a hammer to break them up, since I don't have a mortar and pestle.)

Directions:
Make the tomato soup: roughly chop the garlic then sprinkle with ¼ tsp. salt. Use the side of a large knife to press and rub the garlic and salt into a paste.

In a large pot, heat a splash of olive oil over medium-high heat. Add the garlic paste and tomatoes and sauté, stirring occasionally for 4 minutes. Add the vegetable broth, balsamic vinegar, tomato paste, bay leaf, and season to taste with sugar and pepper. Bring to a boil then lower the heat and simmer, uncovered, for 5 minutes. Take the soup off the heat and remove and discard the bay leaf.

In a food processor or blender, or with an immersion blender, purée the soup until smooth. If it's too thick, gradually add more broth. Season to taste with salt, pepper, and vinegar and stir in the basil and keep warm.

For the topping, heat a small splash of olive oil in a medium, heavy pan over medium-high heat. Add the bacon and cook for a few minutes until crispy and golden brown. Transfer to paper towels to drain. Gently break the bacon into large pieces.

Divide the soup among bowls and top each serving with 2 teaspoons of ricotta. Sprinkle with the bacon, fresh basil, and crushed peppercorns.

BEET SALAD WITH GOAT CHEESE

Salad Ingredients:
1 medium red beet
3 baby yellow beets
½ goat cheese log, cut into ½ inch cubes
1 tsp. finely chopped chives
Salt and pepper to taste

Dressing Ingredients:
1/3 cup olive oil
2 tbsp. lemon juice
1 tbsp. orange juice
Grated zest of ¼ orange
Pinch of smoked paprika

Directions:
Place the beets in cold, salted water. Bring to a boil and cook for about 20 minutes, until tender. (I cut them in uniform pieces when cool enough to handle.) Whisk all the dressing ingredients together until combined. Season to taste. Toss the beets in the dressing while warm, then leave to cool to room temperature. To serve, scatter with the goat cheese then the chives.

RED VELVET CAKE WITH CREAM CHEESE FROSTING

Ingredients:
Cake:
¼ **pound** (1 stick) unsalted butter, plus 1 tbsp. for preparing pans, room temperature
2 ½ cups all-purpose flour
¼ cup unsweetened cocoa powder, such as Pernigotti
1 tsp. baking powder
1 tsp. baking soda
1 tsp. kosher salt

1 cup buttermilk, shaken
1 tbsp. liquid red food coloring.
1 tsp. pure vanilla extract
1 tsp. white distilled vinegar
1 ½ cups sugar
3 large eggs, room temperature

Cream Cheese Frosting:
1 lb. cream cheese, room temperature
½ lb. (2 sticks) unsalted butter, room temperature
4 cups confectioner's sugar, sifted
½ tsp. pure vanilla extract
1 ½ cups chopped toasted pecan halves

Directions:
Preheat oven to 350 degrees. Lightly grease two 8-inch cake pans with butter; line the bottom with a parchment round and grease again. Set aside.

In a medium bowl, whisk together the flour, cocoa powder, baking powder, baking soda, and salt; set aside.

In a large measuring cup, combine buttermilk, food coloring, vanilla, and vinegar; set aside.

In the bowl of a stand mixer fitted with the paddle attachment, beat the butter and sugar on medium speed until light and fluffy, about 5 minutes. Add the eggs one at a time and beat until combined. Using a rubber spatula, scrape the sides and bottom of the bowl as needed. With the mixer on low speed, add the dry ingredients and the wet ingredients, alternately in 3 parts, do not overmix.

Pour half the batter into each prepared cake pan. Smooth the top of each pan with an offset spatula. Place on the middle rack of your oven and bake until a toothpick comes out clean, 30 to 35 minutes. Set aside to cool for 10 minutes, and then remove the cake from pans. Remove the parchment rounds and place on a rack to cool completely before frosting.

Make the frosting: in the bowl of a stand mixer fitted with a paddle attachment, add cream cheese and butter, beat on medium speed until light and fluffy. Scrape down the sides and bottom of the bowl with a rubber spatula. Add sugar and mix with increasing speed until smooth. Scrape the bowl as needed, add vanilla, and beat on high until well combined. Chill in the refrigerator to firm up before using.

To assemble, place a spoonful of frosting on the center of your serving plate and place one cake flat-side-down on top of the frosting. Place four 4-inch wide strips of parchment paper strips around the cake to keep the plate clean and place inside a rimmed baking sheet for easy clean up.

Using an offset spatula, spread enough frosting to create a ¼ inch layer. Place the second cake flat-side-up, (note: if the cake is rounded, use a serrated knife to level it.) Use remaining frosting to cover the top and side of the cake.

Gently press handfuls of chopped nuts against the sides of the cake (the rimmed baking sheet will catch any excess pecans). Remove parchment strips. Serve and enjoy!

Paperbacks & Ebooks for FREE

Go to www.dianneharman.com/freepaperback.html and get your FREE copies of Dianne's books and favorite recipes immediately by signing up for her newsletter.

Once you've signed up for her newsletter you're eligible to win three paperbacks. One lucky winner is picked every week. Hurry before the offer ends!

ABOUT THE AUTHOR

Dianne lives in Huntington Beach, California, with her husband, Tom, a former California State Senator, and her boxer dog, Kelly. Her passions are cooking, reading, and dogs, so whenever she has a little free time, you can either find her in the kitchen, playing with Kelly in the back yard, or curled up with the latest book she's reading.

Her award winning books include:

Cedar Bay Cozy Mystery Series
Kelly's Koffee Shop, Murder at Jade Cove, White Cloud Retreat, Marriage and Murder, Murder in the Pearl District, Murder in Calico Gold, Murder at the Cooking School, Murder in Cuba, Trouble at the Kennel, Murder on the East Coast, Trouble at the Animal Shelter, Murder & The Movie Star, Murdered by Wine, Murder at the Gearhart

Cedar Bay Cozy Mystery Series - Boxed Set
Cedar Bay Cozy Mysteries 1 (Books 1 to 3)
Cedar Bay Cozy Mysteries 2 (Books 4 to 6)
Cedar Bay Cozy Mysteries 3 (Books 7 to 10)
Cedar Bay Cozy Mysteries 4 (Books 11 to 13)
Cedar Bay Super Series 1 (Books 1 to 6)... good deal
Cedar Bay Super Series 2 (Books 7 to 12)... good deal
Cedar Bay Uber Series (Books 1 to 9)... great deal

Liz Lucas Cozy Mystery Series
Murder in Cottage #6, Murder & Brandy Boy, The Death Card, Murder at The Bed & Breakfast, The Blue Butterfly, Murder at the Big T Lodge, Murder in Calistoga, Murder in San Francisco

Liz Lucas Cozy Mystery Series - Boxed Set
Liz Lucas Cozy Mysteries 1 (Books 1 to 3)
Liz Lucas Cozy Mysteries 2 (Books 4 to 6)
Liz Lucas Super Series (Books 1 to 6)... good deal

High Desert Cozy Mystery Series
Murder & The Monkey Band, Murder & The Secret Cave, Murdered by Country Music, Murder at the Polo Club, Murdered by Plastic Surgery, Murder & Mega Millions

High Desert Cozy Mystery Series - Boxed Set

High Desert Cozy Mysteries 1 (Books 1 to 3)

Northwest Cozy Mystery Series
Murder on Bainbridge Island, Murder in Whistler, Murder in Seattle, Murder after Midnight, Murder at Le Bijou Bistro, Murder at The Gallery, Murder at the Waterfront

Northwest Cozy Mystery Series - Boxed Set
Northwest Cozy Mysteries 1 (Books 1 to 3)
Northwest Super Series (Books 1 to 6)

Midwest Cozy Mystery Series
Murdered by Words, Murder at the Clinic, Murdered at The Courthouse

Midwest Cozy Mystery Series - Boxed Set
Midwest Cozy Mysteries 1 (Books 1 to 3)

Jack Trout Cozy Mystery Series
Murdered in Argentina

Coyote Series
Blue Coyote Motel, Coyote in Provence, Cornered Coyote

Midlife Journey Series
Alexis

Newsletter
If you would like to be notified of her latest releases please go to www.dianneharman.com and sign up for her newsletter.

Website: www.dianneharman.com,
Blog: www.dianneharman.com/blog
Email: dianne@dianneharman.com

COMING JUNE 22, 2018

CEDAR BAY COZY MYSTERY

SUPER SERIES #2

Pre-order and save $2.00

http://getBook.at/CBSS2

Italy, Cuba and the Northwest - Travel with Kelly, Sheriff Mike, and their dogs as they search for murderers and the perfect meal. Along the way you'll meet plenty of quirky characters, dogs, and cats. Discover why all of the page-turning books in this series have been designated as best sellers by Amazon. Not to mention that each book has mouth-watering recipes!

From a USA Today and Amazon #1 Chart Bestselling Author comes books seven through twelve in the popular Cedar Bay Cozy Mystery series. Free with Kindle Unlimited.

Open your smartphone, point and shoot at the QR code below. You will be taken to Amazon where you can pre-order the book.

(Download the QR code app onto your smartphone from the iTunes or Google Play store in order to read the QR code below.)

38098221R00093

Made in the USA
San Bernardino, CA
06 June 2019